Even More
SCARY
STORIES
for Sleep-Overs

By Q. L. Pearce

Illustrated by Dwight Been

An RGA Book

PRICE STERN SLOAN
Los Angeles

Copyright © 1994 RGA Publishing Group, Inc.
Published by Price Stern Sloan, Inc.
A member of The Putnam & Grosset Group,
New York, New York.

10 9 8 7 6 5 4
ISBN: 0-8431-3746-0

Library of Congress Cataloging-in-Publication Data

Pearce, Q. L. (Querida Lee)
    Even more scary stories for sleep-overs / by Q. L. Pearce.
        p.   cm.
    Summary: A collection of eleven scary stories.
    ISBN 0-8431-3746-0
    1. Children's stories, American. 2. Ghost stories, American.
[1. Ghosts—Fiction. 2. Short stories.] I. Title.
PZ7.P31495E 1994
[Fic]—dc20   94-2799
                                                        CIP
                                                         AC

Typeset by Carolyn Wendt from a design by Michele Lanci-Altomare

For Kaitlyn Makenzie Pearce

—Q. L. P.

Roger looked out the window. "It's almost dark now," he commented.

"Yeah, I guess I'd better cut through the woods," Juan said.

The boys said good-bye, and Juan set out on the familiar shortcut home. The dismal afternoon was rapidly turning to evening. The shadows under the trees deepened to gloomy pools of black. At least the rain had stopped. The ground was spongy under Juan's feet, and the soggy leaves deadened the sound of his footsteps. He became lost in thought as he trudged along.

All at once, he became acutely aware of his surroundings. Something was different . . . somehow wrong. The air seemed heavier and harder to breathe. He sensed that he was not alone. His ears strained to hear a sound, any sound, but there was nothing. No, there was someone . . . or something coming closer. He squinted into the darkness, and his heart began to pound. He didn't know if he should run or try to hide. In the next instant it no longer mattered. A form stepped out of the shadows.

"Juan?"

He heard his dad's familiar voice and let out a long sigh.

"Dad, what are you doing here?" he asked with great relief.

His father put his arm around the boy's shoulder. "Roger called to say you were taking the shortcut home. I thought I'd come out and meet you. After what happened last night, I don't want you roaming around by yourself. Besides, dinner is ready, and I'm starving!"

The two quickened their pace toward home. They were

unaware of the gruesome thing nearby . . . the thing that was working its way toward Roger's house, the last place where the flute had been played.

• • • • • • • • •

The sound of sirens woke Juan from a sound sleep. Still groggy, he heard another sound, much closer. It was the ringing of a telephone. He glanced at the glowing numbers on the clock radio on his nightstand.

"Three o'clock!" he moaned and rolled out of bed to see what was going on. His mother and father were in the kitchen when he got there, and he heard his father's worried voice.

"Arthur? What on earth . . . ?"

Arthur Peyton lived next door to Roger. Juan watched as his dad's face paled. He seemed to be at a loss for words. He only nodded as the voice at the other end went on. Finally his dad mumbled something, hung up the receiver, and looked at Juan.

"Something terrible has happened. Roger and his folks . . . they . . ." He paused as if trying to find the words. He licked his lips and continued. "The inside of the house was torn up and . . . they're all dead."

All at once it seemed to Juan that the sound of his father's voice was coming from very far away. He heard the words about how Arthur had heard screams and had called the police, but they didn't seem to make sense.

Crying, his mother put her arms around Juan and drew him close. He pulled away.

"I think . . . I need to be alone for a while," he said.

Sitting at the edge of his bed, Juan saw the flute half out of the pack he had tossed on the floor when he came home. He picked it up and thought about how he had been so annoyed when his friend hadn't liked his music. Softly, he began to play. The music soothed him. The flute felt so warm in his hands, almost alive.

Outside in the night, the blood-spattered corpse turned its steps in the direction of the music. It was so near, so very near. The thing's left shoulder ached. Soon it would be whole. Soon it could rest.

Juan continued to play, heedless of the loathsome entity that scraped up the walkway to his home . . . the putrid thing that slowly reached its one arm toward the door.

The Shape of Fear

Barbara stood confidently in front of the class as she gave her report. "The town of Lansford looked as if it had been lifted up from somewhere in Central Europe and plopped right down in the middle of New England. The people of Lansford were very proud of their 'Old World' customs and beliefs. Most of their traditions were harmless, but there was one in particular that was quite bizarre. Some folks believed in the existence of vile creatures known as werepeople, evil beings who looked like humans, but could change their shape at will."

Barbara wasn't at all nervous as she talked. Her family had lived in Lansford since the town was first established nearly two centuries before and she knew more than most kids her age about its history.

"Werepeople, who could take on animal forms and characteristics, were known as shapeshifters. They would use this ability to harm others," she read from her paper. "In the guise of a raven, a wereperson could spy on its neighbors and learn their secrets. As a fox or wolf it could dig up and destroy crops or kill livestock. As a deadly spider or rattlesnake, it could even creep into a home and commit murder, without leaving behind a single clue to its human identity."

Barbara paused and looked around. Everyone was caught up in every word she said. Mrs. Kominski, her teacher, was nodding approvingly. *This is an A for sure,* Barbara thought, glad she had worked so hard on her report. She continued aloud. "While a shapeshifter was in its beastly form, it would not age a single minute . . . and it could not be killed. Only when it was in human form would it grow older and finally die.

"Most people thought that the wicked life of a werebeing was a horrible curse," Barbara explained. "They believed that to become one, you had to be bitten by a wereperson. The bite had to be deep and draw blood."

She lowered her voice dramatically, "But at one time in the history of Lansford, the countryside was plagued by three terrible monsters who had been *willing* prey of a very powerful werebeing. They terrorized their neighbors, and were finally hunted down and killed."

Barbara was very proud that her own ancestor, Jonathan Roarke, had presided over the trials when the trio was finally captured and brought to justice. And the justice of some two hundred years before had been swift.

In a field near the edge of town, stood a huge tree . . . a hanging tree that had supported three sturdy ropes for the accused shapeshifters. The doomed villains had died without confessing the name of their leader, the one who had corrupted them all, but because the vandalism, thefts, and murders had stopped, the search soon ended.

Many modern residents were afraid of the hanging tree, but Barbara was fascinated by it. She could easily see it from her bedroom. In fact, it was so close that sometimes, when the moon was just right, she could see its shadow on the thin, white curtains drawn across her window. Nothing else grew in the field where it stood. Her dad said that there was probably something in the roots that had ruined the soil. Some superstitious townsfolk claimed that the werepeople had been buried there, but no one knew for certain.

"In fact," Barbara said, lowering her papers and whispering to her wide-eyed classmates, "no one knows what happened to the bodies at all!"

"Thank you, Barbara," Mrs. Kominski said. "That was an excellent report. You may take your seat."

After class, Barbara and several of her friends stopped in at the local bookstore to buy the newest issue of their favorite scary magazine, *Tales from Beyond the Grave*. It was displayed on a tall wire rack right beside the front entrance.

"Look at this stupid cave monster," Angela complained. "It couldn't frighten my baby brother. I think the werepeople of Lansford are a lot scarier, and *they* really existed!"

Barbara laughed and shook her head. "No, they didn't. It's just a stupid old story that grandparents use to frighten their grandkids."

"But . . ." Delores began. "What about your report in class? You said that your own ancestor helped to catch them."

"I said he helped to catch three people who were accused of being werepeople and committing crimes," Barbara corrected. "I never said I actually believed they were really shapeshifters. I'll bet old Jonathan didn't believe it, either. That's why he wasn't afraid of them."

Angela tilted her head to one side and asked, "What do you mean?"

"When the bad guys had been caught, Jonathan was the only one brave enough to actually do the hanging and pronounce them dead," Barbara answered with pride. "All the other people were too afraid to get close. They were probably scared of getting bitten!" She lunged at Delores, pretending to bite her neck. Delores squealed, and the other girls laughed.

All at once, Barbara became aware of someone standing near the group. She looked up slowly. A small, thin-faced woman with mournful eyes was glaring at her.

"It is very foolish to make jest of things that you don't understand," the woman warned.

"Jest?" Grinning, Barbara wrinkled her nose and made a funny face at her friends.

"Quite so, Mistress Barbara," the stranger continued scornfully.

The grin faded from Barbara's lips. "How do you know my name?"

A dark smile barely flickered across the woman's grim face. "Think of me . . ." she paused and the smile became almost threatening, ". . . as a friend of the family." She turned and walked quickly out of the store.

"Who was that weird woman, *Mistress* Barbara?" Delores murmured.

Barbara leaned against the large storefront window and gazed in the direction the woman had taken. Except for a couple of young boys wheeling their bikes along, the sidewalk was deserted.

"I don't know," she answered nervously. She had an uncomfortable feeling that she had not seen the last of the odd woman.

• • • • • • • • • •

"It's such a lovely night," Barbara's mom said as she leaned in the doorway of her daughter's room that evening. "Dad and I are going to take a walk. Would you like to come along?"

Barbara glanced up. "No, thanks. I have reading to finish."

Her mom crossed to the bedroom window, pulled back the curtains, and opened it. "At least you can get some fresh air," she said, stroking Barbara's long, brown hair. "We'll be back in a while."

As soon as she was alone, Barbara tossed the book to the floor and got up to reclose the window. She had her hand on the sill when she noticed something that made her stop.

Someone was hunched over beneath the hanging tree. Leaning out slightly, Barbara could just make out the sound of a shovel biting into the barren earth.

"What in the world . . . ?" Barbara muttered under her breath. As she spoke, a silver-rimmed cloud slipped away from across the face of the full moon. Barbara gasped. "It's *her!*"

In the bright moonlight, she could clearly see the woman who had spoken to her in the bookstore. At first it appeared that she might be digging something up, but after a moment, it was plain that the stranger was actually burying a small, dark object. Barbara watched with growing curiosity. Finally the woman completed her task and set off hurriedly along the dirt road that led to town.

Barbara pulled the eyelet drapes closed and stood at the window for only a moment before she made up her mind to see for herself what was hidden away beneath the tree. If she acted quickly, she knew she could slip out and be back before her parents returned from their walk.

Throwing on a sweater, she raced to the garden shed and grabbed a small hand trowel. Within moments she was standing under the twisted limbs of the tree. She had stood in the same place many times before, but never alone at night. The branches cast peculiar shadows on the ground all around her, and when the breeze rustled the dry leaves, the ground almost seemed to be moving as if . . . Barbara shuddered to think about it.

"I'd better get out of here before I start spooking myself," she said aloud. She easily found the place where the woman had been digging and started to work in the soft earth. It wasn't long before the trowel hit something hard. Working rapidly, Barbara unearthed a small, carved wooden box with a plain metal pin and clasp.

Hesitantly, she slipped out the pin, then stopped. She had the eerie feeling that she was being watched. Glancing from side to side, she reassured herself that she was alone. Then, from somewhere in the darkness, Barbara heard a soft rustling noise. *Probably just an opossum,* she convinced herself, but she could barely control the trembling of her fingers as she cautiously lifted the lid of the box.

Moonlight illuminated a small shiny object . . . a tooth . . . some sort of animal tooth on a thin leather strap. It rested on a fragile scrap of paper that appeared to have been torn from a book. As she stared inside, a shadow moved across the contents of the box. Barbara turned her gaze upward and her eyes locked with a pair of glowing yellow eyes. A scream caught in her throat. Crouching on the limb above was a large creature—part wolf, part ferret, part rat. Slowly it edged toward her, clinging to the ancient branch with its long, curved claws.

Clutching the box, Barbara spun around and ran. Reaching the safety of her home, she slammed the door behind her and locked it, then raced to her room. She fell across her bed and tried to catch her breath, then she chuckled to herself.

"This is ridiculous," she declared to the smiling teddy bear on her dresser. "It was only a dumb animal."

She opened the box to examine the contents more closely. Holding the sharp, pointed tooth in the palm of her hand, she took out the folded page and spread it open on her bed. The words were handwritten in a strange language.

"What is this? It looks like Latin or something," she whispered to herself. Slowly, she pronounced each word. Then something . . . a feeling . . . forced her to look up at the drapes drawn across the open window. The light from the full moon had painted a shadowy image of the hanging tree. It danced back and forth as the delicate white fabric moved in the soft breeze. While she watched, three of the horrible creatures like the one she saw in the tree before stole along the lowest branch and dropped to the ground. As if she were in a trance, Barbara's eyes returned to the page. She felt compelled to continue. She had barely spoken the last word, when the first creature crept soundlessly over the sill of the open window. With growing terror, Barbara curled against her pillows as a furred paw gripped the edge of her bed with razor-like claws. The beast drew itself up, and once again, Barbara stared into its glowing yellow eyes.

"It is time," the thing hissed, "to fulfill your part of the bargain, Mistress Barbara. It was most cooperative of you to voluntarily retrieve the box and read the agreement, but then, we counted on your being too curious for your own good."

Barbara had heard the voice before, that very day in the bookstore.

"This isn't happening," she stammered. "I must be dreaming. I didn't make any bargain."

"Oh, but you did. You have just agreed to it by reading the very words that have set us free." Two more of the hideous creatures slipped into the room. "It was promised by your own ancestor, Jonathan Roarke, the werebeing who made us what we are."

"You're lying!" Barbara screamed. "He wasn't a were-person. He killed you."

"No." The beast showed its fangs with a nasty snarl. "He made it appear so. We did indeed give up our human forms and vow to live as animals to soothe the townspeople's need for vengeance. Afterward, your ancestor lived out his life free of suspicion. In return, he arranged for us to have our

freedom in a new time . . . a time when the old beliefs would be considered no more than tales told to frighten children."

Barbara shook her head in disbelief.

"You see," the creature continued, "Jonathan Roarke pledged that in ten generations, his own descendent would take our place. As the time drew near, I was able to appear briefly as a human to carry out the plan."

"NO!" Barbara gasped. "I don't want any part of this."

As she watched, the three creatures began to change. Their limbs stretched outward, and their faces began to take on more human features.

"It is too late!" the woman snarled. "The curse has already been passed to you by the bite of your own ancestor. See for yourself." She gestured toward Barbara's clenched fist.

Opening her hand, the girl saw that the tooth she had clutched in fear, the tooth of Jonathan Roarke, had deeply pierced her palm. Dark red blood trickled down her wrist.

Before her own eyes, Barbara watched her trembling hands shrink into dark, fur-covered paws, and her nails lengthen into powerful claws. She opened her mouth to scream, but the sound was no longer human.

Not far away, on the path leading to their home, Barbara's mother gripped her father's arm. "What was that?!" she cried.

He patted her hand and said soothingly, "It was nothing, dear. Just some kind of animal."

Feast of the Hungry Ghosts

ubo helped his mother hang the last of the tiny, white paper lanterns on the porch.

"There," she said and smiled at her son. "They look beautiful. Our ancestors would be pleased."

The boy groaned. "Mom, our ancestors couldn't care less about whether or not we decorate our back porch."

"Do not be disrespectful," she scolded him gently. "I know you do not see the value in our traditions, but the Feast of the Hungry Ghosts means a great deal to your grandparents. They will only be here for three days. Please try not to spoil it for them."

"But it's stupid to make a meal for dead people and leave

it at the cemetery," Lubo whined. "Especially since our relatives aren't even in the cemetery. They're in China." Lubo shook his head.

His mother gave him a warning look. "That is enough."

Just then a girl with long, dark hair peeked around the side of the house. "Hi, Lubo. Hi, Mrs. Chang," she said, smiling and looking at the lanterns. "Oh, what pretty decorations!"

"Good morning, Zsu Li," Lubo's mom responded.

Lubo grabbed his catcher's mitt and headed for the gate. "Gotta go, Mom. Zsu Li and I will be late for softball practice."

"Come straight home afterward," she called out to her son. "Your grandparents will be arriving this afternoon."

Lubo's family had come to the United States from China, but he had been born here. He was embarrassed by some of the customs they still followed. In particular, he disliked the Feast of the Hungry Ghosts. It is celebrated to honor family ancestors by preparing a special meal and offering gifts to the dead. He and his family would set up the meal at the cemetery and eat right there. When they finished, they would leave food and gifts for the departed.

Lubo was silent as he and Zsu Li walked along, pushing their bikes.

"Your grandparents are coming, too, huh?" Zsu Li sighed. "Mine arrived last night. Are your folks going to make you go to the cemetery?"

"Yeah," Lubo said with obvious irritation.

"I guess it would be different if the graves of our ancestors were here," Zsu Li reasoned. "It's kind of creepy, though, going out to that old cemetery on Gilardi Road. I'm glad we only have to go in the morning."

Lubo nodded. "My dad told me that it's the only place that will allow the ceremonies to be held. There are a lot of families here that still want to do it like they did in the old country, but they don't have a gravesite to go to. Some Chinese families actually have relatives buried there, and they have agreed to share a common area on the grounds with the others. It isn't exactly the same as visiting your relatives, but my mom said that it is the spirit of the celebration that counts."

Zsu Li kicked at a pebble on the sidewalk and watched it skitter into the gutter. "I suppose when our grandparents die, the tradition will die, too."

Lubo laughed. "Well, I'm certainly not going to do it if I don't have to."

· · · · · · · · · ·

When Lubo returned home, his grandparents had arrived. His grandmother was in the kitchen with his mom preparing special dishes, including savory dumplings and tangerine cakes, for the feast the following day.

"Will you be making an offering, Grandson?" his grandfather asked in a formal tone.

"Uhhhhhhhh . . . I guess so," Lubo responded uncomfortably. "I haven't really thought about it."

Grandpa Chang held up a crooked finger and wagged it at the boy. "You would be wise to think about it carefully if you wish your ancestors to protect you from the others."

"What others, Grandpa?" Lubo asked.

Nodding as if agreeing with an unseen guest, the old man

finally answered. "The forsaken ones. They are angry and they seek revenge."

"Come again?" Lubo said, becoming more interested. "You mean like ghosts?"

"Yes, spirits who died without family or were rejected by their family. They become angry at the sight of such festivities in honor of others. These spiteful ghosts wait until darkness falls, then roam in search of vengeance on any living being who ventures out into the night."

Trying not to smile, Lubo cast a sidelong glance at his father, then asked, "And what do they do?"

His grandfather's tone became ominous. "They devour them."

• • • • • • • • • •

"He really believes it, too," Lubo snickered as he told Zsu Li the story the next morning. They were helping to carry the trays from his family's car to their site at the graveyard.

"This place gives me the willies," Zsu Li said with a visible shudder. "You don't think there are any of those angry ghosts around here, do you?"

Lubo rolled his eyes in disbelief. "I don't think there are any kind of ghosts anywhere. There are just a lot of very silly people who believe what they have been told."

He pointed to the crowd of families gathered into small groups. Those with relatives buried in the cemetery were preparing for the ritual beside the graves. Others were setting out their things in a large, central garden. The families whose ancestors were buried elsewhere had taken up a collection to build a decorative pond under a grove of lacy-leafed willows. The pond was surrounded by colorful beds of daisies. Here and there stood stone benches used by some of the older folks to sit and contemplate the meaning of the day.

Lubo knelt to place his tray on the silky, bright red cloth that his mom had spread on the ground. Zsu Li's face lit up when he uncovered the food.

"Wow, ginger chicken is my favorite!" she exclaimed. "Your mom is such a good cook." The aroma of warm chicken coated with a sweet plum sauce filled the air.

"Yeah," Lubo agreed. "But I would prefer to eat this at home—not in the company of a bunch of corpses."

Zsu Li reached down and plucked some thinly sliced ginger from the plate. "A ghost is going to get you for that," she said, laughing as she popped the ginger into her mouth. "I guess I'd better go help my folks. Save me a slice of your mom's tangerine cake."

Within an hour, the formal ceremony was over and Lubo joined Zsu Li at the pond. Along with several other children, she was setting tiny foil-paper boats in the water with an offering of a sweet almond in each one. The slowly sinking boats glittered in the sunlight.

"Did you see some of the things people are leaving here?" Lubo observed in astonishment. "Some of the bowls and trays look like they are solid silver. I saw Mrs. Yee put out a cup that was inlaid with jade!"

Zsu Li barely looked up. "Yeah, this is a very special feast, so those who can afford it really go all out. But they'll come back and pick the things up tomorrow when they're

31

empty, after the ghosts eat their fill."

"Now you're starting to sound like my grandfather. It's more likely that mice and opossum help themselves to the food." Lubo stared into the water for a moment, then a smile spread across his face. "You may have a point, though."

"What do you mean?"

"If a few trays and goblets weren't here in the morning, the old folks would think that their ancestors had taken them."

Zsu Li twisted her mouth into a frown. "Why would the things be missing?"

Lubo grinned. "Because we are going to come back tonight and take them!"

The girl's mouth dropped open. "Are you crazy?"

"Not at all," Lubo said, talking faster as he hatched his plan. "It's a great idea. We could sell the stuff and make a lot of money, and the superstitious old geezers would be thrilled that their offerings were accepted. It's not really stealing. We'd be doing them a big favor."

Zsu Li was not convinced. "But we would have to come back here at night. I don't want to do that."

"Why not?" Lubo taunted. "What are you afraid of?"

"The angry ghosts," the girl muttered, staring at the unattended graves in the oldest part of the cemetery.

"That's just mumbo jumbo, Zsu Li, and you know it," Lubo chided. "Look, no one is going to get hurt."

Still uncertain, Zsu Li finally gave in.

• • • • • • • • • •

Zsu Li let her bike drop to the ground. It hardly made a sound on the soft earth. A half-moon bathed the silent cemetery in a ghoulish blue light. She pushed open the low metal gate that was the only opening in the crumbling brick wall. Warily, she made her way to the pond and called out in a hoarse whisper.

"Lubo . . . Lubo."

Suddenly a figure leapt at her from behind a tree.

"NOOOOOOOO!" she screamed and started to run.

"It's me!" Lubo hissed, grabbing her by the wrist.

The girl was almost in tears. "That wasn't funny," she fussed at him. "Maybe you should just do this by yourself."

"I'm sorry," Lubo said, letting his backpack slip down onto one arm. "You're right. C'mon, we'll be done in no time."

The willow trees cast long, grotesque shadows across the burial stones as the two walked to the first grave. Lubo picked up an ebony bowl and dumped out the vegetables it contained. He studied the empty bowl for a moment.

"Wow, these designs look like they are made out of gold wire. I'll bet this is worth a lot," Lubo said.

"Shhhhhhh! What was that?" Zsu Li whimpered.

From behind them came a low shuffling noise.

Lubo felt the hairs on his neck begin to rise. "I don't know. But it's getting closer."

The two children dropped to their knees and cringed behind a massive gravestone. Moment by moment the noise grew louder. It was the sound of footsteps . . . slow, steady footsteps. The shadow of a figure fell across the stone. Lubo and Zsu Li clutched at each other in terror.

"What are you doing here?" someone demanded in a menacing tone.

"I . . . we . . ." Lubo stuttered, finding it nearly impossible to speak. The figure moved closer, and as it did, Lubo and Zsu Li could see it was a boy, a little older than themselves.

"Why are you here?" the boy questioned sharply. "You've come for the offerings, haven't you? Well, they're mine. You better leave while you still can."

Lubo felt his fear recede like an outgoing tide. It was just another kid with the same idea they had.

"Why should we?" Lubo said confidently. "There's two of us and only one of you."

"Do you know that for certain?" the bigger boy snarled.

Lubo glanced around. He didn't see anyone else, but he decided not to take any chances. "Hey, look," he said to the

stranger. "There's a lot of stuff here—enough for all of us. And this isn't the best of it. I saw a cup over near the pond that looked like it was carved from a single piece of jade."

Moonlight shimmered on the still waters of the pond. The boy hesitated, and then the corners of his mouth turned up in a greedy grin. Without another word, he sauntered in the direction that Lubo had indicated.

As soon as the stranger disappeared behind the trees, Lubo stuffed several items into his backpack. But Zsu Li didn't help. She was staring toward the oldest part of the cemetery.

Her hand trembling, she pointed in that direction. "Look, Lubo!" she moaned. "Something is moving out there. It's them!" Her voice quivered. "It's the hungry ghosts!"

Straining to search the shadows, Lubo, too, saw movement.

"There's something out there all right. That creep really didn't come here alone. Let's go," he urged Zsu Li.

Crouching low, they sprinted toward the cemetery gate. Zsu Li reached it first and tugged with all of her might.

"It's stuck!" she sobbed.

"Let me do it," Lubo ordered, yanking at the thick metal bars. With a squeal, the gate began to open.

"Leaving so soon?"

The two spun around to face the older boy. His face was twisted into a savage expression. "And taking something with you, I see."

With shaking hands, Lubo lifted the backpack up. "Here. You can have it. All we want to do is leave."

The kid stepped closer and grabbed the pack. Opening it, he reached in and pulled out the ebony bowl.

"Okay," Lubo said, trying to control his fear. Over the boy's shoulder he could see the others moving toward them. "You and your friends can have what you want. Now we're going to go." He took Zsu Li's hand.

With an evil grin, the boy raised the bowl over his head and threw it to the ground. It broke into several large pieces.

"We don't want these stupid trinkets!" he howled. "They will not satisfy our hunger." Slowly his body seemed to swirl and expand. Behind him, other phantoms approached, their eyes fixed on the horrified children.

"No!" Zsu Li screamed. "It's true! They're real!!"

It was the last sound that Lubo ever heard.

The Invitation

ven though she had only seen photographs of Aunt Judith, Kaitlyn felt sorry when her dad told her that the old woman had passed away. After all, she was a relative, no matter how distant.

"Why didn't we ever visit her?" she asked.

"She was your grandmother's eldest sister, Kait," he explained. Kaitlyn knew that Grandma Angelica was the youngest in a family of ten children. "They were never especially close," her father continued. "They hardly saw each other even before Judith's daughter disappeared."

Kait looked up with renewed curiosity. "You never told me about that."

Her mom stopped packing clothes into the suitcase that lay open on the bed. "It happened a long time ago," she said. "More than forty years. In fact, I suspect that the reason Judith left her estate to us is because you are about the age her daughter was the last time she saw her."

"I certainly can't imagine another reason," her father commented dryly. "Aunt Judith wasn't any nicer to us than she was to anyone else in the family."

"What happened to her daughter?" Kaitlyn questioned.

Her dad shook his head. "I don't know. It's some deep, dark family secret. Maybe she just ran away. I don't think we'll ever know for certain. But I do know one thing." A smile crept across his face. "If you don't get packed, young lady, you won't be ready for the flight tomorrow. Then your mom and I will just have to leave you here while we check out our inheritance all by ourselves."

Kait giggled. "I'll be ready. What do you think it's like, Dad?"

"I don't know," he answered. "But we'll certainly find out tomorrow."

• • • • • • • • • •

The plane trip from Wyoming to Vermont had been fun, and Kait was enjoying the taxi ride from the airport. They had been driving for almost an hour in some of the most beautiful countryside she had ever seen. Every so often, through wide gaps in the forest of trees that grew almost to the edge of the highway, she caught a glimpse of a shimmering river.

"It's fabulous, Dad," she said excitedly. "Do you think the house is close to the river?"

"The letter said that it was. Look," he said, pointing out the window. "See for yourself."

As the taxi rounded a curve in the road, a rambling, Tudor-style home came into view. It was perched on a small rise that descended in a sweep of grass to the riverbank.

"It's lovely," her mom said softly. "Like a picture postcard."

When the taxi pulled up to the old home, it became clear that the place was not exactly perfect. Even in the deepening twilight, the signs of neglect were obvious. Still, Kait couldn't wait to explore. As soon as her bags were safely in her room on the first floor, she ran outside. Standing on the back patio, she could see the calm, gray-green river snaking along at the base of the rise. An old boathouse that seemed on the verge of collapse extended a short way out from the bank. To the left she could see another small building.

"That must be the carriage house," she said aloud to herself. The lawyer who was helping to settle the estate had told her parents that Aunt Judith had converted the structure to a tiny apartment. A rather surly old man named Howard had lived there for as long as anyone could remember. Howard claimed to have a skin condition that was aggravated by sunlight, so he kept pretty much to himself. But he did have the habit of roaming around late into the night.

It was getting dark now, but Kaitlyn wanted to get a closer look at the boathouse. She started to crunch along the hedge-lined gravel path down the hill.

"Where do you think you're going?" a gruff voice called out, startling her. She wheeled around to face a pale, drawn-looking man. "You have no business out here," he said, squinting down at her.

"I can be anywhere I like," she answered back, trying to appear sure of herself. "My family owns this place."

"So you're the new ones," he snarled. "Well, don't say I didn't warn you." He stomped away toward the carriage house.

"Well," Kait mumbled. "Pleased to meet you, too."

• • • • • • • • • •

Within a week, Kaitlyn and her parents had accomplished wonders with the old estate. It was much cheerier already, so her mom had decided to throw a party to get to know the locals and thank everyone for their help.

Kaitlyn thought it was a great idea. But now, as she helped her mom refill trays of party snacks and listened to the guests talking mostly about the upcoming elections for town council, she lost her enthusiasm. It seemed that no one had kids her age.

Finally, one conversation caught her attention. Kaitlyn settled on the couch next to her dad, who was talking to the woman who ran the dry goods store. She was telling him about the disappearance of Aunt Judith's daughter.

"Actually, she was only the first to disappear," the woman was saying. "Since then, quite a few people have vanished. Oh, sure, many of them were transients. You know, take a job, work for a while, then move on. That could explain some disappearances, but not all. But Judith's girl, well, she was kind of wild." She lifted her eyebrows and looked at Kait.

"Nothing like this dear child here."

Kait cast a glance at her dad that said, *Give me a break*.

"What do you think happened to her?" her father asked, ignoring Kaitlyn and trying not to laugh.

"Well, I imagine she just ran off," said the woman. "There was this circus troop in town . . . a very odd group of people. Never did actually put on a circus. When they moved on . . . the girl was gone, too."

Kait smiled politely. "I think I'll go outside for some air," she announced, heading for the patio. It was a lovely, early summer evening. Kait gazed out at the river and once again the boathouse aroused her curiosity. She had been so busy for the past few days that she hadn't made the time to check it out.

No one would miss me if I slipped away and explored for just a few minutes, she thought.

The door to the old wooden structure wasn't locked, but the rusty hinges squeaked pitifully as she pushed it open. Once inside, Kaitlyn wished she had brought along a flashlight. She could barely make out the shape of the dock that extended into the water.

Kait stood silently and listened to water lapping gently at the sodden timbers. The air smelled of damp earth. She stepped toward the dock and the aging boards creaked under her feet. Suddenly she felt something brushing across her cheek. With a yelp, she jumped back and put her hand to her face.

"Gross!" she said. "Spider webs."

Concentrating on brushing the sticky strands from her hair, she was unaware of the pale hand that reached out

41

toward her from the gloom. The long fingers were only inches from her when she turned her head, hearing her mom calling her from the house. Knowing she really shouldn't be away from the party, Kait scrambled for the door and raced back up the hill.

A moment later Howard stepped from the shadows beside the hedge. He stared toward the main house as Kaitlyn disappeared inside.

•••••••••

The next evening, Kait was curled up in a big, cozy chair near her bedroom window, writing a letter to her best friend. She glanced out to watch the full moon rise grandly over the horizon, then she noticed a small figure near the boathouse. It appeared to be a young girl. Kait quickly opened the heavy, white French doors that led from her room to the patio. She stepped outside to get a better look. The boathouse door was just swinging shut.

"Who could that be?" she asked under her breath.

Grabbing a flashlight from her nightstand, she made her way down to the riverbank. She edged through the open door, switched on the flashlight, and gasped. The beam fell on a girl her own age. She was sitting on the edge of the dock with her bare feet dangling in the cool, dark water.

"I was hoping you'd come," the girl said without turning around.

Kait didn't move. "Who are you?" she demanded.

"Colleen." The girl stood and turned, smiling. "I live in

the big green house just down the river. Do you know it?"

Kait nodded that she did.

"My parents have forbidden me to come here. But when I heard that you had moved in, I just had to. When school's out, there's nobody around here to talk to. I thought, maybe we could just be secret friends. My folks wouldn't have to know."

Kait relaxed and studied the girl for a moment. "Why don't your mom and dad want you to come here?"

Colleen looked down at the water. "Because of all the things that have happened. And because of Howard." She looked up again into Kait's eyes. "He's a vampire, you know," she said seriously.

"What?" Kait couldn't help but giggle. "He's weird all right, but he's harmless. Did your parents tell you he was a vampire?"

"No," Colleen answered solemnly. "Ms. Judith did."

•••••••••

In bed that night, Kaitlyn couldn't fall asleep. She kept thinking about all of the strange things that Colleen had told her. How she had befriended Aunt Judith when everyone else thought she was just a crazy old lady. How Howard had come to town with the circus forty years before, and for some unknown reason had decided to stay. How Aunt Judith had convinced her that Howard was one of the undead and had been responsible for her own daughter's horrible death to satisfy his thirst for blood.

Colleen claimed that the reason Aunt Judith had tolerated

Howard's presence was so that she could gather proof against him. More importantly, she had vowed to find his coffin, burn it, and so avenge her daughter. According to Colleen, once the coffin was destroyed, the vampire's evil existence would end.

"Now that Ms. Judith is gone," Colleen had whispered, "it's up to me to find the coffin and burn it."

"That's ridiculous," Kaitlyn had scoffed. "There's no such thing as vampires."

"If you want proof, you can read all about it in Ms. Judith's private papers," Colleen had assured her. "They're in a small wooden packing chest she kept at the end of her bed."

Before Kaitlyn left the boathouse, she had promised to meet her new friend the following night. Knowing that her parents would be out for the evening, she told Colleen they could meet in the house.

• • • • • • • • • •

At breakfast the next morning, Kait asked her parents if they had seen a packing chest in Aunt Judith's room.

"Yes. It was filled with old papers and books," her dad told her. "It's in the attic now with the rest of her things. Why?"

Kaitlyn smiled sweetly. "I'm just curious about her. Do you think it would be okay if I took a look?"

Her dad shrugged. "Be my guest."

Moments later, Kait was sitting in the attic with the chest open in front of her and piles of papers scattered on the floor. Colleen had been right. The chest was filled with letters, old photos of Aunt Judith and various people, and books on vampire legends, as well as newspaper articles about local disappearances.

Kaitlyn opened a very ornate book and read from one of the pages.

. . . capable of taking many forms such as an animal, or a puff of smoke, but they may not enter a home in any form unless they are invited. The undead are capable of inhuman strength, but they are nevertheless vulnerable. They cannot survive in the light of day . . .

She stopped, remembering how Howard supposedly had a disease that prevented him from going out in the sun. She continued to read.

. . . and a vampire must return to its coffin by sunrise, or cease to exist.

Kait let the book drop to her lap.

"This can't be true." Then her gaze fell on something in the chest that glinted in the dim attic light. It was a small silver picture frame. She took it out and held it cupped in one hand. The frame was decorated with clusters of tiny silver roses, but the glass was broken and the picture was missing. She took the beautiful old frame and a few of the books, thinking that Colleen might want to see them.

· · · · · · · · · ·

That evening Kaitlyn said good-bye to her parents when they left for town, then she opened the French doors in her bedroom. She was busy studying one of the books she had found, when she had the creepy feeling that she was being watched. Looking up, Kait was startled to see Colleen just standing at the open door.

"You scared me." Kaitlyn laughed nervously. "Why are you just standing out there? You should see this. I'm still not sure I believe in vampires but . . ."

Colleen took a step, then suddenly from the darkness outside came a horrible cry.

"NOOOOOOOOOOO!!!!" Howard screamed, hurtling himself at Colleen and dragging her to the ground.

"HELP!" the struggling girl shrieked. "KAITLYN! HELP ME!"

Without thinking, Kait picked up the nearest thing, a table lamp, and threw it at the old man. It glanced off the side of his head. He released his hold on Colleen, and she scrambled away from him.

Rolling to one side, Howard labored to rise to his feet, then he stumbled toward Kait. Blood oozed from a wound on his head where the lamp had struck him.

"Get away from me," she warned. "I know what you are. You're a vampire." Sliding her hands across the nightstand, she found the flashlight and held it up threateningly.

"Please," he moaned, holding out a small square of paper to her. His words rushed out in short gasps. "It isn't me. My brother . . . he was killed by a vampire. It was traveling with that dreadful circus. They were actually protecting it. I found out about them and destroyed the monster, but it was too late. The girl . . . she was already infected by the evil." The old man tried to steady himself against the table. "And all of these years, Judith guarded her, even though she knew what she had become. I . . . I couldn't . . ." His feet buckled under him, and he fell unconscious to the ground.

Kait knelt by his side and pressed a T-shirt to his bleeding head. She looked up at Colleen, who was still standing in the doorway. "We were wrong, Colleen. He's no vampire. Help me."

"What do you want me to do?" Colleen answered in a strange tone.

"The telephone is over there. Call for help," Kait said.

"Are you inviting me in?" asked Colleen, her voice oddly calm for the situation.

"Yes, of course I want you to come in," Kait said frantically. "How else can you . . ."

Just then Kait took the paper from Howard's limp hand. It was a photograph.

She stared in astonishment at the old photo. It was of a fairly young Aunt Judith in fifties style dress. Standing next to her was a girl.

"It can't be!" Kaitlyn gasped, as Colleen stepped slowly over the threshold. "This is a picture of you! But how? Everyone thought you were dead!"

"Something like that," Colleen said, smiling and showing her fangs.

Kait cowered helplessly in the corner. "Stay away!" she begged.

"It's too late," Colleen hissed. "You've already invited me in." And with that, she rushed at the screaming girl.

Camp Colby

Jake stood grinning in the warm, early morning sunshine. He really liked the first day of camp, and he really liked Camp Colby. This would be his second summer here. Nestled on the shores of a crystal-clear lake high in the Sierra Nevada Mountains, Camp Colby had everything. There was horseback riding, boating, sailing, hiking, and plenty of other activities; Jake wanted to do everything.

"Hey, Jake!" someone called.

He turned around and squinted at somebody running in his direction. "Eli!" Jake shouted back, recognizing his friend and bunkmate from the year before.

Eli skidded to a stop on the gravel path. "Did you just get

here? Wait until you see the new boat dock. What cabin are you in?"

"Red Wing," Jake answered.

"Wow. You're kidding. Me too. It's a really cool cabin." Eli gabbed on enthusiastically about how much fun they were going to have, about the horse he hoped they'd let him ride, and about some of the guys he'd already met. "There's a kid named Adam whose dad is in the astronaut program," he said, hardly taking a breath. "Come on, I'll introduce you around."

Jake followed his chattering friend up the steep path to the woodland cabin. It was as cool as Eli had said it was. It had a raised porch in front with a rough string hammock tied between two posts. Inside were six comfortable bunks, and plenty of room for everyone's gear. One by one his bunkmates, Adam, Charles, and Scott, introduced themselves to Jake.

"And I'm Tim," a slightly deeper voice boomed from behind Jake.

Jake turned around to see a tall teenaged boy leaning against the open doorway.

"I'll be your counselor," Tim said with a pleasant smile. "Now, if everyone has put away their things, we have to go down to the cafeteria for orientation. C'mon, let's get it over with so we can really start having fun."

Once all of the kids were seated at the rows of long wooden tables, Mr. Ames, the camp director, explained the camp rules. Jake happily recalled that there weren't very many rules at all, and most were just for safety's sake.

"Finally," Mr. Ames announced, "those of you who have been here before know that this was once a mining area. It's been a very long time since the mine has been worked and it is quite deserted. Still, the entrance to the main shaft is open. It can be very dangerous and I don't want any of you to go near it."

Jake noticed that Tim seemed to stiffen a little and looked strangely uncomfortable while Mr. Ames was talking.

"Is that clear?" the director continued. "That area is off limits," he said sternly, then smiled and changed his tone. "Now, let me end by saying welcome to Camp Colby!"

A general cheer sounded.

• • • • • • • • •

That evening, the kids from Red Wing and two other cabins gathered around a shared campfire. A full moon sailed overhead. One of the camp cooks, a grisly old fellow nick-named Badger, had brought up a supply of hot dogs and marshmallows. He invited himself to join in the cookout, and entertained the boys with funny stories that he made up as he went along.

"Can you make up ghost stories, too?" Charles asked, placing his third hot dog on the end of his roasting stick.

Badger was strangely silent for a moment. The smile faded from his weathered old face. "I don't have to make them up. I know things that happen up here . . . *true* things . . . that would send shivers up your spine."

"Well," Adam coaxed, "like what?"

There was another long pause. Only the sound of the crackling fire broke the stillness. "That mine," Badger rasped and pointed to the black mountaintop silhouetted against the moonlit sky. "One hundred years ago it was turning out enough silver to make everyone involved with it very wealthy. But it was a tough mine to work, so the owners paid top dollar to attract the toughest miners." He raised one eyebrow and looked from listener to listener. "They were a rough, rowdy lot . . . real troublemakers . . . but good miners, nevertheless. There were plenty of brawls, but the men stuck together.

"Anyway, the owners may have paid well, but they skimped in another way. They were more concerned with relieving the mine of its silver ore than they were with the safety of the men. Everyone knew it would happen and it finally did."

"Everyone knew what would happen?" Eli whispered.

"One day old Mother Earth just couldn't take no more poking and digging. You could hear the main shaft groaning all the way in town. Then part of it just collapsed—*CRASH!* No one working the east tunnel made it out. There were more than two dozen men down there. Some people claim that for days afterward, you could hear the sound of their cries from somewhere deep in the belly of the mine." Badger leaned in close to the wide-eyed boys. "Some people say that on a still night like tonight, if you listen real hard, you can still hear the victims of the disaster moaning to be set free."

"Wow!" Jake gasped. "Didn't anybody try to help them?"

"No." The harsh sound of Tim's voice startled the kids. Jake turned to see his counselor sitting a few feet from the fire. The flickering of the flames cast eerie shadows across Tim's face as he spoke. "They just left them there . . . said it was impossible to reach them. I suppose that if the vein of silver hadn't been running out, they might have found a way."

Eli stared out into the night toward the abandoned mine. As if on cue, a coyote howled in the distance. "Have *you* ever heard them moaning?" he asked Badger.

Tim interrupted. "No one has heard them moaning. It's just the sound of the wind in the empty tunnels." He gave Badger a stony look. "The dangers are very real—not supernatural."

That night, as the boys in Red Wing prepared for bed, Scott asked Tim how he knew so much about the mine and why he seemed so angry about it.

"I hate to admit it," the older boy said, "but last year I decided to find out about the mine for myself. So I did a little exploring. I got lost and couldn't find the main entrance. It was just pure luck that I found another way out."

"Weren't you scared?" Adam questioned.

"Oh, sure. The wind really does howl up there. But it's just the wind. That's all. I got a few bumps and bruises, but everything turned out okay. But being in there made me really curious about what had happened to the miners, so afterward I read up on the disaster. It was a terrible thing for those men to have been deserted the way they were. They must have died horribly. I get angry just thinking about it." A dark look crept over Tim's face for a moment, then disappeared. "Look, I'll tell you what. Tomorrow we can all go for a hike up the mountain and I'll show you the main entrance."

Charles shook his head. "Couldn't we get in trouble for that?"

"Don't worry," Tim assured him. "We'll just take a look and come back. Aren't you curious? Besides, you'll be with me, and I guess I know that mine better than anybody."

"Sure," Jake agreed. "What could happen?"

· · · · · · · · · ·

The following morning had dawned drab and overcast. During the first part of the hike the sun had vainly tried to break through, but now it was only a dull disk behind a curtain of clouds. A crisp wind had picked up, too, and the tops of the tallest pines were nodding up and down.

"The sky is really dark over there," Eli pointed to the west. "It looks like a storm is heading this way. Maybe we should go back."

"No," Tim said confidently and kept walking. "It'll probably just blow over. It happens all the time up here in the summer. We're almost to the mine, anyway. Let's keep going."

Within minutes, heavy drops of rain began to splat on the trail around them. Jake pulled a worn baseball cap out of his back pocket and slipped it on his head. "I think Eli is right," he said. "We don't want to get caught out here in a storm." As if in agreement, the sky lit up slightly, followed by an ominous roll of thunder. "If we turn back now, we might make it back to camp before it hits."

But nature had something else in mind. All at once a blazing flash of lightning sizzled directly overhead and a clap of thunder boomed like a cannon. The rain escalated to a downpour.

"Now what?" Charles shouted above the fury.

"We have to take cover," Tim answered, trying to sound

calm. He looked around. "The closest place is the mine. We'll be safe there."

The soil was rapidly turning to thick mud as rivulets of rushing water cascaded down the trail. The boys struggled to follow their counselor. Through the deluge, the opening to the mine loomed into view. It was black as coal and seemed to scar the hillside.

"In there?" Scott hollered as water streamed down his face. "You want us to go in there?"

"It's the safest place," Tim barked back. "I'm going in."

Another bolt of lightning convinced everyone else to follow.

Jake pulled out his flashlight and looked around at the tunnel. "Geez, it's creepy in here. But at least it's kind of dry."

Scott jumped. "Did you hear that?"

"What?" Charles muttered. "I didn't hear any . . ."

"Wait!" Jake cautioned. "Scott's right. Listen."

There was a slight rumbling sound overhead. It was getting louder.

"Get back!" Jake bellowed. The unstable, rain-sodden dirt and rock over the mine entrance gave way. The boys leaped away from the opening just in time before tons of debris quickly piled up, trapping them inside.

When the movement stopped, Jake shined his light on the entrance. The boulders were far too big to move. The boys simply gazed at it, dumbfounded.

"What are we going to do?" Adam whispered. "Nobody knows we're up here. We're never going to get out."

A second flashlight beam flared to life. It was Tim's.

"Don't worry," he said calmly. "Remember what I told

you? I've been here before. I know another way out. We just have to follow the old mine car tracks." He pointed the beam at a pair of iron rails that had been used to move the mining cars loaded with ore.

The boys started to follow, when a unearthly moan sounded from somewhere deeper in the tunnel.

"What was that?" Scott said with a shudder.

"The wind," Tim assured him. "Now let's go."

• • • • • • • • • •

The tunnel was littered with fallen boulders and timbers that had once been used to shore it up. The boys had to pick their way along slowly and carefully. Their only weapon against the oily blackness came from the two slim flashlight beams. Their only leads were the two slender, rusted rails. It seemed that they had walked for nearly half an hour, when suddenly the rails disappeared.

In the circle of light, they could see that this part of the tunnel was partially flooded. The tracks vanished into the stagnant water.

"It's a natural ditch," Tim explained. "It must have gotten flooded since I was here, but it isn't very wide. The tracks are supported by a trellis." Tim stopped as he noticed the worried faces of the campers. "The only way across is to walk on the rails. They must be just below the surface." The boys were silent. "Look, guys. We don't have a choice. I'll go first."

"I don't want to do this," Scott wailed. His whole body was shaking.

Jake put the flashlight in the terrified boy's hand. "We have to," he soothed, trying to keep his voice steady. "Here, you take the light. It'll make you feel better."

Once again, a mournful groan filled the tunnel. "It's the timbers," Tim said firmly. "Let's go." He stepped onto the slippery rail and started out into the water. One at a time, each boy followed. Jake was last, behind Scott. They were only a few feet out when Scott began to wobble.

"There's something in the water," he cried. "I felt something. It's got my ankle!" Screaming, he lurched forward into Charles. Both boys toppled into the murky water. Jake watched in horror as they seemed to be sucked under by some force. The flashlight glowed underwater just long enough for Jake to be certain that he saw *three* flailing figures, not two. Then it went out and the splashing stopped.

"Do something!" he yelled at Tim. "We've got to help them!"

"There's nothing we can do," Tim said, almost without feeling. "Keep going. It's your only chance!"

Slipping and sliding the youngsters sloshed forward.

"We made it!" Adam wheezed as they tumbled onto the soggy tunnel floor on the opposite side of the ghastly pool.

"Don't stop now," Tim ordered.

Eli stayed on the ground. "What about Scott and Charles?"

"We can't help them," the older boy snapped. "We've got to save ourselves."

Tim started down the tunnel. Reluctantly, Adam followed, then Jake. Eli was close behind. To keep from going crazy with fear, Jake listened to the steady crunch of Eli's footsteps in the gravelly soil. We will get out, he said to himself over and over. Then he realized that he no longer heard footsteps behind him.

"Eli?" Jake called out.

No answer.

Jake turned and called again louder. "ELI!" But his friend was gone.

Jake twisted back to see the glow of Tim's flashlight disappear up ahead. He raced after him. Out of breath, he reeled around the corner into a wide chamber. From somewhere high above, an opening was letting in just enough daylight so that Jake could see that they were no longer alone.

At least two dozen wispy figures stood staring at him.

"What are they?" murmured Adam. He was pressed up against the chamber wall.

Some had horrible gashes all over their ghostly bodies. They looked like wounds that might have been suffered as an aging, unsafe tunnel crumbled in on them, crushing their frail, human forms. Others were almost unmarked. The remnants of tattered flesh on their hands, however, was probably the result of uselessly trying to dig a way out of their grave a century before. Somehow, some hideous part of them had remained.

"What's the matter, Jake? Cat got your tongue?" Scott stepped out from behind an outcrop of rock. Charles, too, stepped forward.

Another voice added, "Don't tell me you aren't glad to see your dear friends?"

"Eli," Jake whispered.

"You might say that," Eli answered. He ran his hand over his own chest. "At least this is Eli's body. It feels so good to

be warm again."

Jake turned his gaze to Tim, who stood smiling down from a ledge leading to the opening above. "Tim, what is happening?"

The older boy peered coldly at Jake and Adam and scowled. "Yes . . . *Tim* . . . it was so fortunate that he wandered in here. His body has been so useful. You see, it is the only way we can get out. We need . . . *vehicles,* so to speak. Bodies, to be more accurate. Tim was the first, and now, with this body, we can draw others here. Just as we did with you. Soon we will all be free of this horrible pit."

The phantoms approached as Adam's and Jake's screams filled the dark, dank tunnels.

Tim started to laugh. "Good-bye for now," he said. Then he motioned to Eli, Scott, and Charles. Together the phony counselor and his new cohorts scrambled out of the opening onto a trail leading back toward camp. The rain had stopped and each of the beings gulped in deep breaths of sweet air. Moments later, what had once been Adam and Jake joined them. They looked at each other with knowing smiles and started back toward Camp Colby to recruit more boys for the next day's hike.

The Pact

he old woman rocked back and forth in her chair. Her eyes were not on the three little girls sitting at her feet, but on the dirt road that led toward the swamp. "It devours snakes and gators whole," she was saying with her distinctive Cajun accent, "and if you are brave enough to stay and listen, you can hear its victims' bones snapping like dried sticks." She paused. "But Lakoti prefers a meal of tasty human flesh."

Char turned and looked toward the tops of the giant cypress trees that soared upward from the Louisiana bottomland. She knew that there were plenty of deer, wild turkeys, and even a black bear or two out there. But according to legend, it was also the home of the gruesome man-lizard, Lakoti, that her grandmother was talking about.

"Make the noise it makes again, Gran," she begged.

Char's grandmother pursed her lips and made a strange hissing noise, then followed it by clicking her tongue against the back of her teeth. Char and her friends, Jennifer and Jamie, each tried to imitate the sound, but they couldn't get it right.

"That is the sound of Lakoti breathing in and out between his dagger-like fangs. It is the sound of his razor-edged scales snapping against one another as he slithers in search of prey. If you are unlucky enough to hear that," the old woman warned, "Lakoti is already close enough to have picked up your scent. Few people have been able to escape when Lakoti is that near."

The girls cringed in fear and delight.

"Momma!" Char's mother stood at the open screen door with a scowl on her face. "Don't you be scaring these babies with your silly tales." She turned to Jennifer and Jamie and smiled. "C'mon girls. I promised your folks I'd drive you back to the base in time for dinner."

· · · · · · · · · · ·

In bed that night, Jamie strained to hear the sounds of the swamp through her open window. Her Dad was a career military officer so, even though she was only seven years old, she had already lived in several different places. This was her favorite. And Jennifer and Char were her best friends ever.

Jennifer's parents were also in the military, but Char was a local. She was from a Cajun family that had lived on the bayou since the eighteenth century. Char knew a lot about the swamp and she had shown Jennifer and Jamie some great stuff, like the best place to search for tadpoles and crayfish, and how to spot a raccoon's nest. The girls called themselves the "three musketeers." They even had a secret hiding place, a clearing about a half-mile into the swamp, where they would eat picnic lunches. Jamie wished she could stay in Louisiana forever. That was why the news she heard the following Saturday morning—that they were moving again— was so disheartening.

"You'll make new friends," her mother soothed. "And you can write to Jennifer and Char. Besides, I'm sure you'll like California."

"I know," Jamie said sadly. It wasn't her parents' fault that they had to move. There had been many changes on the base recently. Her dad said it was being "down-sized," and a lot of people were being transferred.

In fact, later that day, Jamie learned that Jennifer, too, would be leaving. Only Char would be left behind. The three girls sat sullenly in their secret meeting place, watching dragonflies buzz at the surface of the water.

"Do you think we'll ever see each other again?" Jennifer finally asked with a sigh.

"Of course we will," Char said sharply. "If you want something badly enough, you can make it happen no matter what." She looked from one girl to the other. "But why don't we make sure?"

"How can we do that?" Jamie questioned.

Char waded out into the muddy water and snapped three sharp spines from the trunk of a water locust tree. "We'll make a pact," she announced solemnly. "A blood pact." And with that she poked the tip of one spine into her finger. A drop of bright red blood welled up. "Exactly five years from today, we will meet in this exact spot . . . no matter what," she continued, allowing the drop of blood to fall to the ground. As it seeped in, she handed Jamie and Jennifer each a spine. They each did as Char had done.

"Then it's settled," Char said. "Friends forever. Nothing will stop us from being together on that day."

"Friends forever," the others responded.

· · · · · · · · · ·

Five years later, standing on the back porch of her new home and looking out at the tops of the giant cypress trees, Jamie remembered the day she and her friends had made their sworn pact as if it had only been yesterday. It was as though fate had been working to help the three girls keep their promise. Her dad had not expected the transfer back to Louisiana, but here they were. And only one week before the appointed time.

Jamie wondered if Jennifer and Char would be there, too. At first the girls had kept in touch with each other by writing regularly. After a while, though, the letters had become fewer and farther between. In fact, it had been almost a year since she had heard from either of her friends.

"Jamie?" a familiar voice said softly.

Jamie turned to see Jennifer framed in the doorway. "I can't believe you're really here!" Jennifer cried, running to her friend.

The girls laughed and hugged each other. "My mom told me that your family had been transferred, too," Jamie said. "How long have you been here? Have you seen Char?"

"I've been here about a week," Jennifer answered. "But Char isn't here. I guess you didn't hear about the accident."

"What accident?"

"It happened about a year ago. Char's mom and grandmother were killed in a car accident. She was sent to live with a relative . . . a cousin, I think . . . in New York."

"I'm so sorry," Jamie said mournfully, remembering how kind Char's family had been to her. "I'll miss them. Do you think Char is okay?"

Jennifer shrugged. "It's been a long time, but maybe she'll be able to come back to meet us." Suddenly her face brightened. "I have an idea! Mrs. Willis is still at the post office. She would know how to reach Char. We could get an address where we could write to her and let her know we're back. We still have a week to go. Maybe she could get here. She said nothing would stop her!"

"Fantastic!" Jamie agreed. "I have to go to the post office with my mom today. I can write the letter and mail it!"

• • • • • • • • • •

Finally, the time to fulfill their pact had come. Jamie glanced at her watch, then back to the picnic basket that she and

Jennifer had prepared before making their way to the special clearing. There was a chill in the air and a light mist rose from the sun-warmed water. In the distance, a few bull frogs were practicing their evening chorus. Finally Jamie spoke.

"We don't know if the letter even got there, Jen. I'm sure she would have been here if she could." She rose to her feet and put a hand on Jennifer's shoulder. "We shouldn't stay any longer. It'll be dusk soon. We haven't been out here in ages. I don't think I could find my way back in the dark without Char."

Jennifer smiled. "Yeah, and we wouldn't want to be stuck in this part of the swamp alone. Remember old Lakoti?" the girl said, then tried to imitate the funny hissing, clicking noise that Gran had made so convincingly.

Jamie noticed the shadows lengthening on the ground as the sun crept closer to the horizon. "You still can't do that very well," she said, laughing as she bent down to pick up the basket. Then a soft sound broke the surrounding hush. It made Jamie stop laughing. It actually made her shudder.

Hsssssssss . . . click . . . click . . . click.

Jamie straightened up and looked at her friend. "Wow! I'm really impressed. That was much better." But Jennifer was staring out over the swamp toward a shadowy grove of white oak and bald cypress trees. Lacy strands of Spanish moss hung from the branches and dangled into the water like cobwebs.

"That wasn't me," Jennifer said with a tremor in her voice.

"Oh, come on . . ." Jamie began, but she stopped when she saw the look on her companion's face. "Let's get back," she murmured.

The girls walked in silence for a few hundred yards. The mist was getting strangely thick and warm. Then suddenly they could go no farther. A tall stand of vegetation that looked like feathery bamboo blocked their path.

"Canebrake," Jamie muttered to Jennifer. "We must have made a wrong turn. I don't think we should try to work our way around it. In this mist I can't tell how far it goes."

Before they could take another step, the strange hissing noise echoed over the water once again, followed by a series of clicks. It was closer than it had been before.

"It's Lakoti!" Jennifer moaned in terror. "He's picked up our scent."

"Don't be ridiculous!" Jamie countered, but she couldn't stop her hands from shaking. "It's a gator. Lakoti is . . ." But she didn't finish. Everything was eerily quiet. Even the bullfrogs had stopped croaking. Through the haze she could barely make out a dark shadow rising from the swamp. The girls backed toward the canebrake as the form loomed closer, then seemed to disappear. The sound of something moving in the water broke the stillness . . . something very big. The air smelled foul and Jamie found it almost impossible to breathe.

"Don't move at all," she whispered to Jennifer. "Maybe it will . . ."

"YEEEEEAAAAAAGGGGGGHHHHHHHH!!!!!!" Both girls screamed in horror as a huge creature leapt at them in a surge of foaming swampwater. At least ten feet tall, it leered down at them with gleaming yellow eyes. Clumps of slime hung from its long, sickle-shaped claws.

"RUN!!" Jamie shouted, pushing Jennifer ahead of her.

Both girls sprinted in the direction from which they had come. Tripping over a protruding root, Jamie fell hard to the ground and rolled. The beast was close behind, howling in anger. Its huge mouth was lined with dripping fangs, and its long, forked tongue whipped around as it roared. It was almost on her.

"GET UP!" she heard Jennifer shriek. Then suddenly she felt someone tugging at her arm. Scrambling to her feet, Jamie charged after her friend.

Crashing into the clearing, the girls searched their surroundings from side to side in despair. "There's nowhere to go!" Jennifer cried.

"THIS WAY!" someone yelled.

The two girls snapped their attention to a small rise and saw Char motioning them on.

"There's no time! HURRY!" Char shouted.

In panic, the three girls clambered up the side of the small hillock and tumbled down the other side. The soggy ground shook beneath their feet as the bloodthirsty monster galloped after them. Char darted toward a tall stand of swamp red maple. The trees grew close together and their gnarled roots and buttresses stuck out at all angles like knobby knees.

"Lakoti's too big to follow us in here," Char gasped.

Up to their hips in a dark, murky pool, the girls held their breath and pressed themselves against the gray-green trunks. "Duck down as far as you can into the water," Char instructed. "That way Lakoti won't be able to pick up our scent."

The girls did as they were ordered. Jamie felt her feet

sinking in the muck. Something slick slithered along her leg, and she fought the impulse to scream.

All at once, the nightmarish beast sloshed into view. Tiny waves splashed against her face and stung her eyes, but Jamie could still see the creature swinging this way and that. It was so close that she could smell the stench of its fetid breath.

Then, to her surprise, Lakoti bellowed in rage and headed deeper into the swamp.

Char made a silent sign to the others not to move. As the thrashing of the creature faded away, she motioned for her friends to follow her.

Without a word, the trio made their way out of the hellish swamp as quickly as their feet would carry them. Once back on the road toward the base, the shivering girls hugged each other in relief.

"How did you . . . when . . . ?" Jamie stammered at Char with trembling lips.

"I said that nothing would stop me from being here." Char smiled. "I couldn't let you two city kids fend for yourselves out in the swamp."

Jennifer shook her head. "I never really thought that Lakoti existed. I still can't believe that this happened. We've got to tell somebody . . . to warn them."

Char shook her head. "The people who live on the swamp know deep in their hearts that the legends are true. The others . . . well, you will never convince them no matter what you say." She took Jennifer's and Jamie's hands in her own.

"You are my very best friends," Char continued. The

important thing is that you made it. No one else ever has to know what happened here."

Jamie nodded. "You're right. This will be our secret. We can talk about it more tomorrow. Right now I'd like to go home and get out of these wet clothes."

"Friends forever?" Char asked.

"Friends forever," Jamie and Jennifer answered.

· · · · · · · · · ·

At home, Jamie slipped off her soggy shoes and snuck quietly in through the kitchen door. She was sure she would never be able to give her parents a believable explanation about why she was soaked to the bone. Tiptoeing through the front hall, she noticed a letter addressed to her on the hall table. It had Char's return address in New York on it. Jamie picked up the envelope and padded to her room. She slipped out of her wet clothes and into a bathrobe, then she pulled out the letter.

I guess Char wanted to let us know that she was coming, she thought, tearing it open. She read a line or two, and then drew in her breath sharply. The envelope slipped to the floor. The letter was from Char's cousin. It was short and matter-of-fact. Jamie stared at the last lines.

The accident occurred three months ago. It was such a terrible shock so soon after the similar deaths of her mother and grandmother. If it is any comfort, she was killed instantly and certainly did not suffer. If there is anything else . . .

71

The letter continued. But Jamie could no longer read through her tears. Char had truly meant it when she had said nothing would stop her from being there on their appointed day . . . not even the grave.

"Yes, Char," Jamie sobbed. "Friends forever."

By Any Means

asha stood defiantly in front of Robbie. "You pushed me in front of the ball!" she said angrily.

"Get real," the accused boy said, gloating. "You jumped right in front of it. The name of the game is dodge ball. You got hit, so you're out."

"But you cheated, Robbie Jefferson," she whined again.

"So what else is new?" called a kid on the sidelines as he elbowed his buddy. "I'd be really surprised if he didn't cheat."

The other children laughed. Robbie also smiled as if he had just been given a compliment.

"The idea," he informed them, "is to win. How you win is not as important."

73

The bell rang and all the kids filed into Mr. Juarez's classroom. As Robbie and the other kids took their seats, Mr. Juarez placed small stacks of papers on each desk in the front row. Then he instructed the person sitting at that desk to take a paper and pass the rest back.

"Okay, settle down now," he ordered. "We are going to have a quiz today on the King Arthur and the Knights of the Round Table story we read."

A low groan rumbled through the class.

As soon as everyone had a test paper, Mr. Juarez gave the signal to begin. For nearly twenty minutes, the class was quiet except for the scratch of pencils and the occasional rub of an eraser, as each child answered the questions.

Cautiously, Robbie wriggled in his chair until he was able to see the paper of the boy in front of him. Julian was a straight-A student, and Robbie never missed an opportunity to take advantage of the seating arrangements.

"Cut it out," Julian whispered hoarsely as Robbie eventually leaned closer to get a better look.

"C'mon," Robbie coaxed. "What's the difference?"

In answer, Julian hunched forward over his quiz, blocking the other boy's view.

· · · · · · · · · ·

After class, Robbie stopped Julian near the bike rack. "You're a real jerk," he said. "I don't see how it can hurt you if I get a couple of answers off your test."

"It hurts everybody," Julian shot back angrily. Several

kids paused to listen to the argument. "But especially you. You'll never learn anything that way."

Robbie grinned smugly. "My dad said I could go to the County Fair this weekend if I got an A in English. That's what really matters."

Julian shook his head. "You may think you're getting away with something, Robbie. But you're going to end up looking like a fool, just like King Arthur's court jester."

The next day, Mr. Juarez handed back the graded tests. The day after that, Robbie cornered Julian outside. "So what do you think now, genius?" Robbie said with a smirk. He waved a ticket to the fair in Julian's face.

"I still think you're a fool," Julian replied.

• • • • • • • • • •

Everyone had looked forward to the opening of the County Fair for weeks. It had everything! There were special exhibitions, pie-eating contests, pig races, and a haunted house. There were rides, too, including the county's tallest Ferris wheel and a roller coaster known as the "bone-crusher."

Robbie and his friends, Josh and Ted, spent much of their time on the midway. Now, with evening settling in, the game booths were all lit up with flashing colored lights. For a quarter you could try your luck at popping balloons with darts, or tossing baseballs at milk bottles. If you did well enough you could win a really cool prize. Robbie had his heart set on winning a laser sword. It was a big, plastic saber that glowed dull yellow in the dark and made a neat whistling noise when you raised it over your head.

He had already spent five dollars in quarters in his quest for the prize when he saw Julian and a few of his friends making their way through the crowd. Robbie was about to turn away, when something grabbed his attention. Tucked under Julian's belt was a laser sword!

"So where did you steal the sword?" Robbie challenged as he and his friends swaggered over to the group of kids.

Julian narrowed his eyes for a moment, then answered calmly. "I won it fair and square. I know that's hard for you to understand, but—"

"What's so great about winning a dumb sword?" Robbie interrupted. He turned to Ted and snickered. "A two-year-old could win one of those."

"So why don't you have one yet?" Sasha asked.

"I'm planning on winning something much better," Robbie boasted.

"I'll believe it when I see it," Julian scoffed.

Robbie was getting furious. "Okay, how about if we have a contest? Let's meet back here in an hour and we'll see who has won the best prize. The loser pays ten bucks." He held up a ten-dollar bill. "Your sword doesn't count because you already have it. The contest has to start from now."

Julian frowned. "I can't. My folks are expecting me home in thirty minutes."

"I thought so," Robbie said, sneering. "You're afraid I'll beat you."

"No way! I accept the challenge *if* we do it tomorrow."

"You're on!" Robbie said, offering his hand. "Shake on it." The two boys shook hands.

As Robbie and his friends walked away, Josh gave him a disgusted look. "Are you crazy? You haven't won anything yet and you tried all afternoon! How are you going to win this stupid bet?"

Robbie scowled. "It wasn't important enough before. Now it is. I always find a way to get what I want."

"Yeah, we all know how you usually win, but it's going to be hard to cheat on this one," Ted pointed out, gesturing toward the midway. "None of the bozos in those booths are going to just *give* you a big prize."

Robbie whirled around and glared at his friends. "Look, jerk, I said I'd do it and I can do it without you. Why don't you just get lost?"

Without another word, Josh and Ted stormed away. Robbie stood alone on the bright, gaudy midway as a happy crowd milled around him, but he wasn't in the mood to smile. His friends were right. Slowly he started to move away from the throng and toward the softly lit side exit.

"Hey, kid," someone called from the shadows beside what appeared to be an empty booth.

Robbie peered into the darkness but couldn't see anyone. Lowering his gaze he took another step.

"Hey, kid. Wait." A tall, thin man now stood half in and half out of the light. He was dressed like a clown, but the expression on his face was more sinister than funny. "I couldn't help but overhear your problem, and I can help."

"How can *you* help?" Robbie said rudely.

"I have something you want." The man pulled on a cord, which raised a curtain in the darkened booth. Robbie's eyes opened wide. There was a lavish display of toys . . . stuffed

unicorns and dragons with glittering eyes—magnificent models of armored knights on horses—and in the center of it all was an incredible toy sword. It glowed with its own silvery light, and gems of different colors winked on its hilt.

"I can assure you that you will win the prize of your choice here tomorrow in full view of your friends if . . ." The man hesitated, making sure he had Robbie's attention.

"If what?" Robbie asked impatiently.

"It's quite simple. On either side of this booth there are gates that lead to a maze. All you have to do is enter the first gate, then make your way through the maze before the second gate closes, and you win."

"How can I be sure that I'll make it . . . and what's in it for you?"

The man stroked a small goatee on his chin. "Let's just say I enjoy the sport of it," he said. "I like to play the game. Meet me here tonight at midnight, and I will let you try the maze for yourself. That will give you an advantage over the others."

"That's cheating," Robbie said, smiling.

"Perhaps it is," said the man. "Perhaps it is."

• • • • • • • • • •

Sneaking out of his house was easy for Robbie, and it wasn't any harder to climb over the chain link fence that surrounded the fairgrounds. He dropped quietly to the ground and rose to his feet. It all looked very different now. There were no bright lights. There was no music blaring. The booths were closed with wooden shutters and secured with heavy padlocks.

Listening to the sound of his own footsteps as he crept down the darkened midway, Robbie began to think that this wasn't such a good idea. All of a sudden the lights on the carousel flared to life. The music began to play and the splendid horses bobbed up and down as the huge machine started to turn.

Rooted to the spot, Robbie watched in alarm as the strange carnival man came into view. He was holding on to one of the brass rails. With a wicked grin he leapt to the ground and bowed to the boy.

"Welcome," the man said dramatically.

The carousel immediately dimmed and the music ground slowly to a halt.

"How'd you do that?" Robbie asked in astonishment.

The man winked. "An old carnival trick. Come. It is time for our little game."

Robbie remained silent and followed the stranger to the open gate at the mouth of the maze. When he finally spoke, his voice faltered. "I've been thinking. This is kind of weird . . . no . . . it's too weird. I don't think I want to do it after all."

"But you have so much to gain," the man hissed. "All you have to do is make it through the maze." He gave the boy a sharp push and slammed the iron gate shut.

Robbie twisted around and threw himself at the closed entryway. "And if I don't make it?" he called out, his voice shaking. "What happens if I don't make it?"

The man's answer seemed to echo from everywhere and nowhere. "Why then, of course, you will stay . . . forever!" Horrible laughter rose all around the terrified boy, now pounding at the door.

"NOOOOOOO!!! Let me OUT!!" screamed Robbie.

"You are wasting precious time," the man said calmly.

Then all was silent. Fearfully, Robbie turned and studied the dark passageway ahead.

"Calm down, Robbie," he told himself under his breath. "The guy is just wacko." He held out his hands and groped along step by step. The passage separated into two different paths and he chose the turn to the right. "All I have to do is follow the wall and everything will be . . . YEEEEEEEAGGH!!" Robbie howled as the ground dropped out from under his feet. He felt himself falling, then he came to a sudden stop that knocked the air out of his lungs. Catching his breath, Robbie saw that he was in a cavern that was lit by a reddish glow. He stood warily and looked around.

"Why is it so warm in here?" he muttered. The wide passage curved away to the left where Robbie saw an opening in the opposite wall. With mounting terror, he dashed toward it. All at once the floor of the cavern shook beneath his feet. It was then that he realized he wasn't walking on dirt and stone. He was walking on something alive! First one huge, snake-like head rose high into the air and swayed above him . . . then another. Each head had fiery red slits for eyes, and each open mouth housed gleaming, needle-sharp fangs.

The first head struck at him and Robbie rolled out of range. Without hesitation, he jumped to his feet and raced for the opening. He dove into it just as the second head released a burst of searing flame.

At first Robbie slid helplessly along, then the passage leveled out and he found himself at a fork in the maze. Knowing that there wasn't much time left, he sprinted to his left and slammed into something. Reeling from the crash, he looked up into a nightmare. An eyeless skull grinned at him. The skeletal body was encased in a rusting suit of armor and the thing held a huge silvery sword in its fleshless hand. Beyond the phantom, farther down the passage, Robbie could see a glow. It was the gate. Its iron hinges squeaked ominously; it began to swing shut.

"NOOOOOOO!!!!!" Robbie wailed. He charged at the ghastly sentinel and it raised its sword high, leaving a small unprotected gap on one side of the passage. Robbie's legs felt as if they were on fire, but he aimed for the tiny avenue of escape just as the sword came whistling toward him.

• • • • • • • • • •

"I could have told you Robbie wouldn't come. He was just too chicken to show up," Sasha declared while opening a fresh package of cotton candy. "He knew he couldn't win the bet fairly. Why don't we just go ride the bone-crusher?"

"You're right," Julian nodded. "Robbie is such a fool."

As the kids walked away, an odd-looking man with a small goatee on his chin chuckled to himself while he hung a large stuffed toy for display in his booth.

"Right you are," the man laughed aloud, adjusting the costume of his new jester doll. "Right you are."

Looking remarkably like Robbie, the jester's face had a foolish-looking painted-on smile, but its unseeing eyes were forever frozen in an expression of horror.

The Power of the Mind

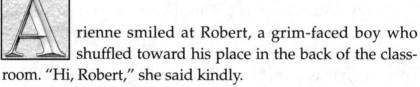rienne smiled at Robert, a grim-faced boy who shuffled toward his place in the back of the class-room. "Hi, Robert," she said kindly.

Jill leaned over from across the aisle and whispered, "I don't understand why you're nice to that know-it-all creep." She watched him with obvious distaste as he slumped into his seat.

Arienne reached under her desk and took out her reading book. "Oh, he's not so bad. Showing off how smart he is is his way of getting attention." She shrugged her shoulders. "I don't let it bother me. Besides, he doesn't have any friends. I feel kind of sorry for him."

Jill wasn't convinced. "Well, I think he's a class A weirdo. It runs in the family."

"That isn't a very nice thing to say," Arienne replied sternly.

Jill rolled her eyes. "Maybe not, but you know it's true."

Arienne had to admit that Robert was a little strange. And everyone in town knew that his great-grandfather, Jedediah Gray, had been committed to a mental institution, and that he died there. Still, Arienne believed that it was cruel of the kids to tease Robert about it, but he did have a knack for getting on everyone's nerves.

Just as the bell rang, Mr. Cutter hustled into the room, balancing an armload of books and papers.

"Good morning, class," he said, dropping the load onto his desk. He pushed his slipping glasses back into position. "How many of you know what a myth is?"

Several of the kids, including Robert, raised their hands.

"Okay," Mr. Cutter said, "for the rest of you, myths are made-up stories about heroic people, legendary places, or supernatural creatures. Today we are going to read a story about a mythical creature called a basilisk, a beast that was half giant snake and half rooster."

Laughter rippled through the class. Robert, however, didn't crack a smile.

"Don't laugh," the teacher cautioned. "This horrible monster was said to have had poison breath that could destroy anything it touched." He leaned forward and lowered his voice to a throaty snarl. "And one glance from its evil eyes could turn any living thing into clay."

"Stone," a chilling voice from the back of the room

announced with precision.

Mr. Cutter looked up in irritation. "What?"

Robert stared at the teacher, huffed impolitely, and repeated to himself: "Stone. The gaze of the basilisk turned people to stone."

Peering at the boy over the top of his glasses, Mr. Cutter grumbled, "Oh? You seem to be quite sure of your facts, Mr. Gray. Are you personally acquainted with a basilisk?"

Most of the kids burst into laughter.

Red-faced, Robert stared hard at his hands, now clenched into tight fists in his lap.

Later, during lunch, Arienne found Robert sitting alone just outside the cafeteria. "Are you still angry?" she asked softly, leaning against the red brick wall of the building. "Mr. Cutter shouldn't have embarrassed you like that. I guess he was upset because you corrected him so rudely in class."

"That doesn't give him the right to make fun of me," Robert answered. "And to make everyone laugh at me," he added quietly.

"No. It doesn't. But maybe if you tried a little harder to—"

"Oh, no!" gurgled Joe Washington, one of their classmates. He and a couple of other boys were nearby, heading into the cafeteria. "I just saw a basilisk!"

To the delight of his friends, Joe held his arms at his sides, stiffened his body, and pretended to turn to stone.

"You're an idiot," Robert mumbled.

"And we all know what you are," Joe shot back angrily. He turned to his friends, crossed his eyes, and used one finger to make a small circling gesture near the side of his head.

Snickering, the group of boys moved on. Arienne cast a

glance at Robert. He was trembling with anger. "You're not very funny," she called out to Joe. "I think you're—" But she stopped when a sudden movement near the top of the brick wall caught her eye and turned her attention upward. A decorative concrete eagle perched at the corner of the building was vibrating. As she watched, a crack in the base appeared and the stone bird shuddered and slowly toppled forward.

"Look out!" Arienne screamed.

Joe jerked back in surprise, and the statue crashed to bits on the sidewalk right in front of him.

"Wow," one of the boys murmured. "That was close."

Turning quickly to Robert, Arienne was shocked to see that he was smiling.

"You know what, Arienne," Robert said slowly. "Maybe you're right. It was rude of me to correct Mr. Cutter in class. It would be much more effective for him to learn by experience. Perhaps he should examine the basilisk for himself." He threw his jacket over his shoulder and sauntered off, whistling tunelessly.

"But it's a myth," Arienne said aloud to no one. "It doesn't exist."

• • • • • • • • •

When Arienne walked into class the following morning, it was plain that something was wrong. The principal, Ms. Wareham, and Mrs. Gaudio, a substitute teacher, stood solemnly at the head of the class. When everyone was seated, Ms. Wareham spoke.

"I'm afraid I have some very grim news," she said in a hushed tone. "I'm deeply sorry to say that Mr. Cutter passed away last night." The students sat in stunned silence. "Mrs. Gaudio has agreed to take over your class."

All day Mr. Cutter's sudden death was all everyone talked about. Then, after school when Arienne was leaving, she noticed a knot of children gathered around Carrie Lewis, the police chief's daughter. Out of curiosity, she joined them.

"It was too weird," Carrie was saying. "My dad told my mom that they found Mr. Cutter curled up in a corner of his backyard. And he was only wearing pajamas . . . no robe, no slippers."

"Geez," Jill exclaimed. "It must have been below freezing last night. Why would he go out like that?"

"Who knows?" Carrie said. "Since a lot of furniture was turned over, my dad thinks that there was some kind of a struggle and Mr. Cutter ran outside to get away. But that's not the strangest part." The girl lowered her voice to a whisper and the other children leaned in closer. "There was something wrong with Mr. Cutter's skin. It was really dry and hard. And you know what else?" Everyone held their breath while waiting for the final detail. "My dad said he'd never seen a more scared expression on a dead man's face in his whole life. He said he'd never forget it as long as he lived."

As the other kids chattered excitedly, Arienne let Carrie's words sink in. "There was something wrong with his skin . . . dry and hard." *Like stone?* she wondered. Suddenly a terrible thought came into her mind. Could Robert have had anything to do with what had happened to Mr. Cutter? Across the playground she could see Robert and Joe. They appeared to be arguing again and it looked serious. Joe grabbed Robert's jacket and the two boys tugged at it for a moment. Finally Robert wrenched the coat free, whirled around, and ran.

Shaking her head, Arienne set off for the library to do some research for a report she had to do for school. When she got there, Arienne wasn't surprised to see Robert at a table in the reading room. He was hunched over a large book as if he were in a trance and didn't notice as she walked up behind him. His jacket—with a ripped sleeve—was slung over the back of his chair.

Arienne noticed that his total attention was on an illustration in the open book. She slipped closer and peered over his shoulder. It was a frightful drawing of a scaly, winged dragon. Its lips were curled back over long, ghastly fangs, and tongues of flame poured from its flaring nostrils. Robert's hand rested on a second book, a small leatherbound volume on the table beside him, and he seemed to be muttering something over and over under his breath.

Arienne felt a chill of fear snake up her spine. Without a word, she edged away and left the library.

· · · · · · · · · ·

"Did you hear what happened?" Jill cornered Arienne as soon as she arrived in class the next morning. "It's just so gross! The police discovered a body a couple of hours ago. It was fried to a crisp and stuffed up at the top of the big, old water tower out by the refinery. Carrie says it took them over an hour to get the body down and they still don't know who it is."

Arienne focused for a moment on the empty desk where Joe Washington usually sat, then she shifted her gaze to Robert. She watched as he calmly ran his fingers along a freshly mended tear on the sleeve of his jacket.

Mrs. Gaudio began the morning lesson, but Arienne couldn't concentrate. Over and over she said to herself that it wasn't possible. She was being ridiculous. How could Robert have anything to do with these terrible events? But her thoughts kept returning to the horrible dragon she had seen him studying so carefully.

After school, Arienne attended the meeting of her science club. This afternoon they were discussing science projects to enter in the youth display at the State Fair, but she barely paid attention.

"What do you think, Arienne?" she heard as if the voice were coming from a great distance away.

"What?"

Jill had slipped into the seat next to her. "I said, what do you think about doing a model of a volcano? Are you all right? You haven't heard a word I've been saying."

Arienne stood and gathered up her books. "I'm fine. There's just something I have to do. I'll see you tomorrow." And with that, she briskly took off.

Fifteen minutes later, Arienne was standing on the sidewalk in front of the three-story town library. The old building appeared ominous in the fading light of an early mid-winter evening. Still trying to make up her mind, she surveyed the intricate designs around the massive front door. The library had been built in the early thirties and it was adorned with an array of gaudy decorations and carvings that were popular at that time. At the side of the building, a sweeping outdoor stairway led to a third-floor patio, where evil-looking gargoyles guarded each corner of the building. Setting her jaw firmly, she strode up the steps. As she had expected, she found Robert at a table in the otherwise deserted reading room. The same mythology volume and small leather-bound book were in front of him.

"Why?" she said firmly, more as a demand than as a question.

Without the slightest trace of surprise, Robert looked into her eyes. He knew exactly what she meant.

"They deserved it," he responded bitterly.

Arienne felt her jaw drop. She had hoped that she was wrong about Robert, but now she knew her suspicions were true. A jumble of thoughts and fears reeled through her mind, but all she could say was, "How?"

"Hate is a very powerful thing," Robert said simply. "My great-grandfather knew that. He realized that if it could be channeled properly, it could be used as a weapon. It's all here in his diary." The boy tapped the cover of the small book. "He didn't have the powers of concentration to make it work. But I do!" he snapped with sudden fury. "And whatever I imagine becomes real for as long as I concentrate." He spoke with such force that Arienne flinched.

"You've got to stop this, Robert," she pleaded. But he only laughed. "If you don't, then I'll find a way to stop you."

"What can you do?" he grinned, stepping closer.

Arienne began to back away. "I'll go to the police."

"Don't be stupid. They won't believe you." He softened his

voice and reached out his hand. "You are the only person who has ever been nice to me. I don't want to have to hurt you."

Twisting away, Arienne marched to the library doors and down the front steps. Outside it was already quite dark, and the shops and businesses were closed for the night. The empty sidewalk was dotted with pools of light from the glowing streetlamps. She paused for a moment, then turned in the direction of the police station. High above, at the corner of the library rooftop, a grotesque stone gargoyle trembled slightly. Its eyes sparked to life, like glowing embers, then it stretched its enormous, bat-like wings and leaped into the air.

Arienne walked faster as she became aware of a soft whirring noise above. At her feet she saw dried, dead leaves skitter along the sidewalk as if pushed by a breeze. The air began to press in on her, and a voice deep inside screamed a warning. Without looking up she began to run.

Only a few yards overhead, the gargoyle let out a piercing screech and spread its glistening talons for the attack. Arienne felt something smash into her from behind and went sprawling onto the ground. She twisted her head just in time to see the creature beating its inky black, leathery wings against the cold night air. As it turned, she saw the horrible red gash of a mouth opening to expose its stabbing fangs.

"No . . . NO!!!! Stay away from me!" she screamed. Springing to her feet, she dashed toward the town square and dove under the cover of a small white gazebo meant for picnickers. Her breath came in short, shallow gasps as she huddled in the tiny structure, but it was no use. The demonic creature plummeted with full force on the fragile roof, and splinters of wood shot in every direction. Crying hysterically,

Arienne covered her ears, but she couldn't block out the beast's hideous shrieks.

She bolted from the crumbling gazebo and scrambled into a hiding place under a holly hedge. The sharp spines of the leaves tore at her face and hands as she crawled, but it was worth it. The enraged creature continued to claw at the ruined gazebo and hadn't noticed her escape. Quickly creeping out from the holly hedge and keeping to the shadows of the buildings, she made her way back to the library.

"Let me in!" she wailed, tugging on the brass handles and banging on the huge wooden doors, but they were locked. From somewhere in the darkness she heard the cry of the gargoyle getting closer. Frantically she looked around . . . the outside stairway! If she could make it to the third level, she could smash one of the library windows that faced the patio and crawl inside.

Sobbing, Arienne lurched first up one flight, then another. When she reached the third floor, her heart sank. Heavy wooden shutters were securely locked over each of the windows.

"I warned you."

Arienne whirled around to see Robert standing near the edge of the patio.

"I really am sorry," he said. Then he cupped one hand to his mouth. "She's here, my pet!" he called out into the night.

With a bloodcurdling howl, the savage gargoyle swooped down. At the last second Arienne pressed her trembling body against the wall, avoiding the attack. Robert wasn't as lucky. The edge of the beast's wing hit him in the shoulder. Crying out, he toppled over the low safety rail and plunged to the ground below with a grisly thud. All at once, the night was so still that Arienne could hear the pounding of her own heart.

• • • • • • • • • •

"Tsk tsk tsk," the head librarian clucked to her young assistant the following morning. "It was such a tragedy. But I've told everyone we need to put a gate across that stairway and lock it up at night. The poor boy must have slipped . . . and you should hear the story the little girl is telling . . . gargoyles and dragons . . . probably thinks she'll get into trouble if she tells the truth." As she spoke, the woman looked around the reading room and her voice took a harsher tone. "Look at this mess, Andrea. Why haven't you shelved these books yet? If this job is too difficult for you to handle I can always find someone else, you know."

"I'll take care of it right away, Mrs. Jordan," her assistant mumbled, trying to hide her anger. The older woman always seemed to find fault with everything. Picking up a mythology book from the reading room table, Andrea read the number on the spine, and slid it into its proper place.

"See that you do!" Mrs. Jordan ordered and walked away.

Next Andrea picked up a small leatherbound volume from the table. "Someday I'll find a way to teach that old battle-axe a lesson," she muttered. Absentmindedly, she flipped open the little book and began to read.

Family Reunion

Peter searched the landscape as it whizzed by. "Water tower!" Pete called out excitedly. "Water tower starts with W. Now it's your turn." He glanced slyly at his big brother, Mark, who was sitting in the backseat beside him. "You have to find something that starts with X."

To pass the time on the long car ride from Phoenix to King City, Missouri, the family had been playing an alphabet game. The object was to take turns finding something that started with each letter of the alphabet. His mom and dad had lost interest somewhere around Q, but Mark had stuck with it. Although they were ten years apart in age, Mark was very patient and attentive to his younger brother.

Mark studied the farmland whizzing by outside the van window. "X-tra big cow," he finally announced with a straight face.

"That's not fair!" Pete shot Mark a glance. But he wasn't really annoyed.

"Okay, I give up. You win," Mark said as he tickled Pete in the ribs. "There's no way I'm going to see a xylophone out here."

It was a long drive to the family farm to visit Uncle Ed, Aunt Belinda, and Grandma Ruby. Pete had been there several times before, but this time was different and very special. It was the ten-year family reunion. At the last reunion he had only been a baby, so he didn't remember any of it. He'd certainly heard about it, though . . . a lot.

"There have been Collinses on this land since the Louisiana Purchase," his dad had always said proudly. Mark had actually been born there before their parents moved to Arizona. Now, family members were coming from all over the country to gather in the small midwestern village that was their ancestral home. Pete was going to get to meet aunts and uncles and cousins that he'd never met before, including Uncle Milo. He was the oldest person in the entire family. As they drew closer and closer to King City, Pete could hardly sit still.

• • • • • • • • • •

When the road-weary group finally pulled up to the large, white farmhouse, Uncle Ed was standing on the porch with a big grin to greet them.

"Well, it's about time you got here," he boomed in a deep voice. "Belinda's been staring out the window since lunchtime."

As he spoke, a pleasant-faced woman in her mid-fifties appeared and waved enthusiastically from the kitchen window. By the time the family was inside, Aunt Belinda was already setting out a hot meal in the dining room.

"Land sakes!" she declared, laughing heartily. "You must all be starving."

Chatting and laughing, everyone took a seat at the table. It was obvious, however, that there was one empty place.

"Where's Grandma Ruby?" Mark asked.

Belinda and Ed shared a serious glance. "She's just feeling a little under the weather," Ed said finally.

"I'm fine." Everyone looked up to see the plump, gray-haired woman standing in the doorway. She stared back at them without smiling. "It's all this fuss," she complained. "I just can't stand it. All these folks coming here. Why can't they just get this business over with quietly and go home?"

"Hi, Grandma Ruby," Pete said, surprised at her gruffness. Usually she was so nice whenever they paid a visit.

The old woman turned and walked away down the hall without responding, but not before Pete had noticed her throat and the backs of her hands. They were covered with patches of dry, scaly skin.

Belinda quickly launched into an apology. "Grandma Ruby's not feeling herself, but she's going to be 'seen to' very soon." Pete noticed that his mom and dad were nodding knowingly.

"C'mon, Champ. Get a move on or I'll get all the pancakes," Mark said the next morning as he and Pete rolled out of their beds.

"Not if I can help it!" Pete laughed, racing to grab his jeans.

Moments later they clambered into their places at the kitchen table. Still laughing, Pete bumped the table as he sat down and a little orange juice slopped over the side of his glass.

"Can't you boys behave like gentlemen for once instead of hooligans," Aunt Belinda snapped. Everyone looked at her in surprised silence. Nervously, she used her napkin to dab at the small spot of juice on the tablecloth. Pete couldn't help but notice the small, dry patches of scaly skin on the backs of her hands.

"I'm sorry," Pete said timidly. He tried to change the subject. "Is Grandma Ruby feeling better this morning?"

With a grim expression, Belinda looked at the other adults at the table. "She's . . . not well. She's gone away for a day or two."

"Away where?" Pete asked.

"Just away!" his aunt answered harshly. And with that she stomped out of the room.

Pete and Mark spent the early part of the day in town, and Pete was glad since everyone at home seemed kind of grumpy. Still, almost everywhere they went, they ran into a relative, and it didn't take long for Pete to realize that most of them were edgy and out of sorts, too. When he and Mark got home, Pete decided to talk to his parents about it. He found them in the living room going over some sort of printed schedule or timetable.

"He should be ready by tomorrow," his dad said seriously.

His mom was somber. "How do you think we should handle it?"

"We'll leave that to Milo."

When Pete entered the room, they stopped talking and his dad slipped the timetable into a large, plain envelope.

"What's up, son?" he asked with a forced smile.

Pete flopped down into an overstuffed chair by the picture window. "What's wrong with everyone?" he asked. "I thought this was supposed to be a big celebration, but no one seems very happy."

"Well," his mom began, "there are so many things to do, family traditions and all. People get irritable."

A knock on the door interrupted their conversation.

"Why, I wonder who that could be?" Mr. Collins said with a false cheeriness.

It was Uncle Milo. If there was a center to the entire family, he was certainly it. Pete had no idea how they were related. *Everyone* called him "Uncle." All of the adults treated him with respect and—Pete thought—fear.

As Milo stepped inside, Pete felt his spine tingle. The old man looked like a walking corpse. His dry skin hung in loose wrinkles on his face, and a few white hairs stuck straight out from his age-spotted scalp. No one knew for certain how old he was. He had run the huge storage warehouse at the edge of town for as long as anyone could remember.

"George . . . Monica," Milo said gruffly as he nodded a greeting.

Pete felt anxious as the aged man turned his dark gaze directly on him. Without a word, Milo grasped the boy's hand and ran his bony fingers over the pink flesh.

"Almost time," he wheezed under his breath.

Pete was so transfixed by Uncle Milo that he barely noticed when Mark entered the room.

"Uncle Milo," Mark said, extending his hand. Milo took it and gazed at it intently. Finally he looked up and smiled like a hideous cadaver.

"Yes. This is good. You come with me to the warehouse, boy," Milo ordered.

Mark obeyed without question. He didn't even look at his little brother as he followed the old man out of the door.

"Why are they going to the warehouse?" Pete said mostly to himself. He stood at the picture window. As he watched the pair leave, he absentmindedly rubbed at a patch of itchy red skin on the back of his hand.

· · · · · · · · · ·

A bright bar of sunlight falling across his pillow awakened Pete early the next morning. Rolling over, he noticed that Mark's side of the bed had not been slept in.

"He didn't tell me anything about a fishing trip," Pete said scowling when his mom explained where Mark had gone.

"Well, maybe he doesn't tell you everything," his father snapped angrily.

Pete didn't believe their explanation for a minute. His parents had never lied to him before. There was something going on, and he intended to find out what. Whatever it was, it had something to do with that warehouse.

· · · · · · · · · ·

With late-night shadows darkening its time-worn walls, the warehouse looked creepy and distorted. It hadn't been difficult for Pete to sneak out of the house after everyone else had gone to sleep, but now it didn't seem like such a good idea. Taking a deep breath, he hoisted himself up through a partially open window. Once inside, he could tell why no one had bothered to lock the windows. The place was filled with broken-down farm equipment that looked like it hadn't been used in years. Some of the rusty hulks were partly covered by tarps, which made the junk look like huge, crouching beasts waiting to spring.

Suddenly Pete heard a scuffling sound near the wall to his left. He switched on the small penlight he had brought with him and aimed the beam in the direction of the noise. A large pair of rat eyes glared back at him. The creature's greasy-looking fur shimmered in the dim light. It took a step toward him, then another. Pete glanced from side to side for a way to escape, but the rat abruptly turned and slinked away.

Pete let out a long sigh and bounced the thin beam around the area where he stood. On the far wall, he noticed a door. He moved quietly toward it, gripped the handle, and slowly turned it. The latch clicked and he pulled the door open to find a wooden staircase that led down into the blackness.

"Okay, hero," he said softly to himself. "I guess this is what you have to do."

Pete squared his shoulders and took a step . . . then another. Even though he was scared, he descended step by step into a huge, vault-like underground chamber. As in the room above, there were tarps covering objects. He edged toward the object closest to him. Extending his trembling hand, he gripped the edge of the tarp and pulled it back.

"YEEAGGGGGHHHHHH!" He stumbled backward away from the ghastly sight. There on a smooth, metallic table lay the body of a man. It was wrapped in what looked like a coating of sticky threads, not unlike those of a spider's

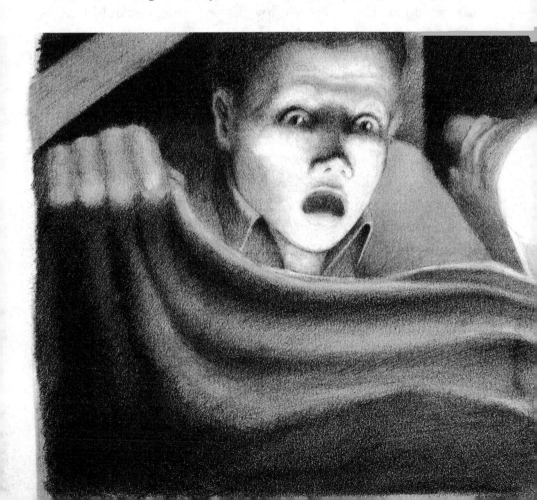

web or a moth's cocoon.

Gathering his courage, Pete lifted up the tarp he was now leaning against. It was another body.

"I don't believe this," he gasped. In the beam of his small flashlight, he could see dozens of covered tables. He reached out and lifted one more tarp. Tears blurred his vision. Mark's unseeing eyes stared back at him. He, too, was covered by the sticky layer of stuff.

"NO!" Pete cried out, touching his brother's face. It was cold and clammy.

"We didn't expect you so soon, son." A pair of incredibly strong hands grasped Pete from behind and lifted him off his feet. It was Uncle Milo.

"What have you done to them?" the boy screamed, kicking and trying to free himself from Uncle Milo's grasp.

"I'm sorry you had to find out like this," the old man said calmly. "But it's too late now. We'd best get you home."

With an iron grip, Milo guided Pete toward the now well-lit farmhouse. His frantic parents were waiting inside. The boy stared in disbelief. They looked as if they hadn't slept in weeks. His mother scratched continuously at the scaly skin of her arms and face. It peeled away in long, dry strips.

"Where did you find him?" his dad asked with agitation.

"In the warehouse," Milo growled. "He knows."

"Oh, for heaven's sake, Milo," a gentle voice interrupted. "He's got to find out some time."

Pete snapped his attention to a figure standing at the hall door. It was Grandma Ruby. She looked younger and lovelier than he had ever seen her. She smiled sweetly and held out her arms to him.

"Come here, child. Everything is all right."

Milo pulled Pete's sleeve back to expose the boy's arm. His skin was peeling in parched sheets. Terrified, Pete twisted out of Milo's grasp and backed toward the door. "Get away from me!"

"Peter," his mother soothed. "Please . . . you have to . . ."

Pete's heart was beating like a hammer. "What are you doing?" he screamed. "What happens? Do the old people take over the bodies of the young? Is that it?"

From the corner of his eye, Pete saw Uncle Ed trying to slip into the room from the kitchen. Pete wheeled around and zigzagged between his father and Milo, barely escaping out the open front door.

Keeping to darkened fields and away from roads, Pete managed to get away. With tears stinging his eyes, he stumbled through tall standing rows of ripening corn. Finally, drawn to the glow of an all-night gas station just off the interstate, he lurched onto the blacktop and stood blinking in the glaring lights.

"Help me," he begged a young man who was filling the tank of his brand-new sports car. "Please, I need a ride into the city."

"Sure," the man shrugged. "I'm going that way anyway."

On the road, Pete settled back in the passenger seat and let his mind wander. He had to get to the police, but what could he tell them? Whatever he decided, it had to be soon. He paid no attention to the direction the car was traveling until a huge eighteen-wheeler passed them on the road. The lights from the truck lit up the face of the young man driving the car. For the first time Pete noticed the shreds of dry skin peeling from the man's neck.

"What?" Pete sat up straight just as the car pulled in behind the warehouse. "Let me go!" he screamed at the stone-faced man who dragged him from the seat. He struggled, but he couldn't break free. Once they were in the underground room, the man released him. Fists clenched, Pete cringed under the steady gaze of Uncle Milo. To his horror, he saw that his mother was lying on one of the metal tables. A thin layer of the sticky material covered her like gauze and she was breathing heavily.

She opened her mouth to speak in a labored voice. "Don't fight, Peter. It is our way."

Strangely, Pete was suddenly calm. Maybe she was right.

Turning his head slightly he saw an elderly man being helped from a table. The man looked as if he was awakening from a gentle slumber.

Uncle Milo placed a strong hand on Pete's shoulder as the boy watched his father take his place on one of the tables. "It must be," Milo said gently. "When our home world was destroyed two Earth-centuries past, this planet was the only place we found where we could survive." As the old man spoke, Pete felt a growing sense of serenity. "By hiding the truth about our origins, we have been able to live peacefully among the earthlings without detection. That is all we have ever wanted. But we are not exactly like them. The energy from this sun causes our outer layers to . . . let's say . . . wear out. To survive on this planet, every ten years, those of our race must experience a resting period, a time of change."

"You mean sort of like a butterfly?" Pete questioned.

A familiar voice said, "Something like that."

Pete looked up at Mark. As his older brother helped him to a waiting table, Pete felt a sticky substance being released from his own skin. A soft, threadlike cocoon started to form.

"This is the time that we are most vulnerable. But don't worry. You're not alone." Mark assured him. "We gather together here to guard each other. It won't take very long, then we can all return to our homes and the earthlings will never discover our secret. It will be easier for you the next time."

Pete nodded, closed his eyes, and allowed himself to drift into a deep, restful sleep.

Nightmare on Sugar Dome

ody groaned as he rolled over in bed and looked out of the window. It was a perfect day. The air was clear and the morning sunshine made the deep layer of snow on the ground sparkle. In the distance, Sugar Dome, the state's finest ski area, was a gleaming invitation.

Cody looked at the book bag on the chair next to his bed. "Why do I have to go to school on a day like this?" he grumbled aloud and tunneled under his down comforter.

Maybe you don't have to, a little voice in his mind suggested. Peeking out from under the covers, Cody grinned. He had an idea. He hustled out of bed and into his clothes. Then he shoved a pair of ski gloves and goggles into his book bag.

He'd have to rent skis and poles, he thought, retrieving a cigar box from his dresser drawer. He counted out some of his birthday money, slipped the cash into his pocket, set his face in a serious expression, and went downstairs.

"Morning, Dad," he said innocently as he slipped into his place at the table and picked up his glass of juice.

"Hey, kid," his father smiled. "What a great day, eh? The sort of day that makes you want to play hookey!"

Cody swallowed his juice a little too fast. "Yeah, I hadn't thought about it," he lied, coughing. "You're right."

His mom laughed. "Dream on, guys." She glanced at her watch. "Look at the time! Cody, Dad, and I have an early appointment. Do you want us to drop you off at school?"

"No, thanks, Mom," he answered. "I'll take the bus."

Cody was already standing at the bus stop at the end of his street when his parents drove by on their way to their real estate office. He smiled and waved. But once their car disappeared around the corner, he stepped behind the tall hedge that grew along the sidewalk. Stashing his books under the bushes, Cody waited until the big, yellow school bus rumbled by. He boarded the next city bus for Sugar Dome Ski Lodge.

The lodge was a great place. There was a video arcade on the lowest level, and the snack bar served the best curly fries and hot chocolate in the world. The main hall had a gigantic open fireplace and a fantastic view of Sugar Dome. Cody stood in front of the huge glass wall and gazed up at the sun-drenched mountaintop. Perfectly groomed ski runs snaked upward through the trees. Dozens of brightly dressed skiers zigzagged back and forth down the slopes.

"All right!" Cody declared to no one in particular. To one side of the run he could see the alpine tramway that carried skiers all the way to the peak. From where he was standing, the heavy cable that supported each of the silvery gondola cars looked like flimsy thread vibrating in the breeze.

For just a moment, Cody felt a strange chill and the light around him seemed to dim. A sensation of panic knotted his stomach. But the creepy feeling vanished as quickly as it had come, and Cody made a beeline for the rental shack.

"Hey, Tracey," he called to the tanned young man behind the counter. "How about a favor?"

"What are you doing here, Cody?" his friend asked. "Isn't this a school day?"

"Uhhhhhh, yeah . . . but I had a doctor's appointment this morning, so my folks let me take the rest of the day off," Cody answered. "I thought maybe you'd let me try those new skis you were telling me about."

Tracey bought his story, and soon Cody was crunching through the snow toward the tram. He waited on the platform with a few other people as the car bumped to a stop. The ground operator unhooked the latch and slid the doors open. The car was large enough for a dozen people. A metal handrail encircled the inside and there was a storage rack attached to the inner roof of the car.

"Have a good run," the operator commented pleasantly to the group as he reclosed the doors.

When the latch clanged shut, Cody felt the same strange chill he had experienced earlier. But then, with a loud hum, the car began its ascent high up the face of Sugar Dome.

Cody studied the other passengers. To his left was an

elderly couple in matching blue ski jackets. A woman with a long blond ponytail and a tangerine-colored jumpsuit was talking to an odd-looking man who had a cast on his right wrist. The guy gave him the creeps. Cody glanced to his right and met the gaze of a dark-haired girl about his own age. She was with a man and a woman who were most likely her parents. *They must be here on vacation*, Cody thought, smiling shyly at the girl.

THUMP!! A loud noise sounded from somewhere above them. "What was that!?" the girl with the ponytail cried in alarm. Before anyone could answer, there was a grinding sound and the car lurched back, swinging from side to side. One more bump sent Cody hurtling across the car. His head slammed into the handrail, and everything went dark.

When Cody came to, everything was still dark. It took him a moment to realize that a large blanket had fallen from the rack above his head and covered him. Pushing it aside, he sat up and looked around. The empty car was stopped at the mountaintop station with its doors open.

"Thanks for leaving me here, folks," he muttered to himself. Rubbing the spot where he hit his head, he gathered up his equipment and stepped out of the car. The platform was empty. *I guess the others were in a hurry to get out and didn't see me there*, he thought. He stepped into his skis and glided across the packed snow next to a man getting ready to start down the hill.

"Looks great, doesn't it," Cody observed. The man took off without saying a word. Cody made a face. Setting his own poles, he pushed down until he felt his skis sliding forward. The crisp air felt wonderful as he picked up speed.

By skiing to an uncrowded rope lift about midway down the slope, Cody was able to ride up and ski down several times. He was enjoying himself so much that he forgot all about the dull throbbing in his head.

Cody was heading across the hill, when a patch of orange in the trees caught his eye. Crunching the edges of his skis in the snow, he stopped. A figure in a bright, tangerine-colored jumpsuit was standing half-hidden in the undergrowth at the edge of the run. It was the woman with the blond ponytail and she was staring right at him. She had some kind of dirt— maybe a huge, dark bruise—on one side of her face.

The glare from the sunlight made it hard to see into the shadows. He skied in a little closer.

"What in the . . . ?" Cody looked this way and that, but he saw nothing but pine trees. The woman was gone. He turned back toward the run and almost bumped into a man standing beside him. A broken cast hung from the fellow's right wrist and he held his head at an odd, tilted angle. The man opened his mouth as if to speak, but nothing came out. In frustration, he reached out and gripped one of Cody's ski poles.

"Hey, let go! Are you nuts?" Cody yelled. He yanked the pole away and took off down the hill.

Upset by the man's strange behavior, Cody stuck to the middle of the slope. He decided not to make another run.

•••••••••

"Thanks, Tracey," he called out to his friend as he set the borrowed equipment against the wall in the rental shack.

Engrossed in what appeared to be a serious conversation on the house phone, Tracey didn't even look in his direction.

"Oh my God!" Tracey said into the receiver. "When did it happen? Does anybody know who was in it?"

When did what happen? Cody wondered as he shuffled back outside. The day was becoming overcast and the breeze had turned icy. The interaction with the bizarre guy had made him nervous. He jingled some quarters in his pocket and walked toward the video arcade. Inside, the noise and the crowd made him feel better. Taking up a place at one of his favorite games, *Invasion Force from Alpha 5*, he dropped a quarter in the slot.

"Yeeeesssssssssss!" he exclaimed when he had downed the last alien spacecraft. Then something drew his attention from the game: The dark-haired girl from the cable car was leaning against the far wall watching his every move. The commotion of the arcade faded to a soft buzz. It was almost as if everyone else in the room was dissolving away. All he could see were her coal-black eyes.

"What's going on?" Cody said aloud. He closed his eyes and opened them again. The girl was gone. Cody gasped in disbelief, but she had simply vanished.

Confused and frightened, Cody tried to refocus on the game, but when he shifted his gaze, his heart leapt with terror. Standing behind him, reflected on the glass screen, was the scowling face of the man with the cast. Stunned, Cody saw the image reach out toward him. In panic, he dodged the outstretched fingers and bolted for the door.

Once outside he raced toward the main hall entrance, then skidded to a halt. The elderly couple he had first seen on the tramway stood glaring down at him from the huge window wall. Their blue jackets were stained with dark red blood. Turning on his heels, Cody dashed along the now slushy path, splattering clumps of wet snow as he ran.

"Tracey!" he gasped as he burst through the doorway of the rental shack. "I don't know what's going on. I need your help!" But the young man ignored Cody.

"I can't believe it," Tracey said softly to another man who was leaning against the counter. "He was only in here a couple of hours ago."

"TRACEY!" Cody screamed.

"He can't hear you."

Cody snapped his head up to see the man with the cast standing in the open doorway. One by one, the other passengers stepped into the shadowy room. Cody looked from one to the other.

"We can't leave without you, boy," the man whispered.

The boy cringed and covered his eyes. "No . . . I don't believe you. . . . No. I'm going to open my eyes and you'll all be gone. This isn't really happening." As he spoke, Cody felt the ground grow cold. He opened his eyes and found that he was kneeling in the snow near a pile of twisted metal and broken glass that had once been a cable car. High above, a snapped cable twisted in the wind.

Painfully he watched as a stretcher was loaded into a special ambulance. The small body on the stretcher was completely covered with a heavy plastic material.

"It's so heartbreaking," a nearby paramedic noted sadly. "I know his parents. They probably think he's in school."

Backing away, Cody sensed that the others were near

him. He looked up into the eyes of the man he had been so afraid of, but all of the fear was gone.

"It's time to leave," the man said simply.

Another cable car slowly appeared and the doors slid silently open. Cody watched the ambulance pull away, then stepped into the car. The doors closed and the car faded into the gathering mist.

Danger Island

There were a lot of reasons why tourists visited Lake Wintoma. Decker Island, however, wasn't one of them. It was a small, bleak circle of land just off the far eastern shore of the otherwise gorgeous lake.

The island was, more accurately, a peninsula, but even during the dry season, the boggy tongue of land that connected it to the mainland was usually under two inches of water. The townspeople called it "Danger Island" because of the hazards it posed. Incredibly overgrown, the place was a haven for snakes and insects . . . and Dr. Rowan Decker.

Dr. Decker was a paleobotanist, a scientist who studies ancient plants, and he was the only person who chose to live on the peninsula. He had settled there twenty years before, and had built a secluded home. For the most part he kept to himself . . . except on the first and third Saturdays of every month. On those days he made the hour-long drive around the lake to the town on the west shore, to stock up on supplies. During his visits, he regularly stopped for a snack at the corner diner where he was often joined by several of the local kids. He entertained them with strange tales of his wordly travels. Decker knew about all kinds of bizarre things, and he would captivate the kids for hours.

One day he was in town talking to John and his friends, Rodney and Bethany, about a strange plant he'd come across in his studies, called the rafflesia.

"It is the largest flower on the planet . . . about three feet across," Decker said, spreading his arms to show the size.

"It must really be beautiful!" John said in awe. No one he had ever met told better stories than Dr. Decker.

Decker curled up his lip in a playful smile. "Well, that's a matter of opinion. You see, many people claim that the rafflesia flower smells an awful lot like rotting meat."

"Oh, come on," Bethany scoffed, wrinkling her nose. "What kind of flower would smell like that?"

"One that was pollinated by flies," Decker answered seriously. "They *like* the way it smells! But I've seen even odder things," he continued.

"Like what?" Rodney asked.

The scientist leaned forward. "Like plants that eat meat . . . plants that strangle the life out of other plants . . . and a gooey, plant-like lifeform that can move from place to place!"

John frowned. "I've read about meat-eating plants, like

Venus's-flytrap. They trap insects between their leaves and then dissolve the bodies for food. They're not all that special. But I've never heard about the others. Are they for real?"

Decker nodded with assurance. "They're real all right. In fact, I have samples growing on the island. The strangling fig, for example, is a vine that climbs over and eventually chokes a host tree. It usually grows in rain forests, but I've had luck transplanting such vines to several areas near my lab."

"What about the gooey thing that moves?" Bethany asked.

"Slime molds," Decker answered. "Yes, they grow here. They're found in damp, dark places . . . like under a log . . . or perhaps a basement. A slime mold consumes tiny living things, such as bacteria, by enveloping them."

"Cool!" John exclaimed. "Like the Blob in the movies, that creature from outer space."

"Yes. But if my theories are correct, these things were even more impressive in the past. Perhaps, millions of years ago, a distant larger relative of the modern slime mold had a taste for much bigger game." A faraway look settled on Decker's face. "We could learn so much about how life on Earth developed if we could study those ancient plants. The work would be dangerous—the plants might be difficult to control —but it would be worth it. I have worked hard to genetically peel away the centuries. And I am *very* close."

• • • • • • • • •

A week later, on the school playground, John crept up behind Bethany, who was sitting on the lawn, engrossed in a book. In

119

his hand he cradled a container of tapioca pudding. Bethany didn't notice John until he tipped the pudding onto her hand and yelled, "The Blob that devoured San Francisco! It's here!"

Bethany jumped up, screaming, and flicked the gooey mess from her hand, while John and Rodney shook with laughter.

"You idiots!" she yelled, trying to suppress a smile.

"The attack of the mutant slime mold begins," Rodney snickered, handing her a paper towel from his own lunchbox.

"Sorry we scared you," John said, unwrapping his sandwich. The three kids ate their lunch and talked about everything from soccer practice to homework, but eventually the conversation drifted back to Dr. Decker and his weird plants.

"I'd love to see Dr. Decker's slime mold," said Rodney. "I wonder what he meant by 'bigger game.'"

"Humans," John said, laughing.

There was another moment of silence as everyone munched on their sandwiches. Then John had an idea.

"Maybe we *could* see the slime mold," he said excitedly.

"What do you mean?" Bethany mumbled with a mouth full of peanut butter and jelly.

John rubbed his chin. "We could visit Dr. Decker's lab."

"But he never lets anybody come to the island," Rodney said matter-of-factly. "You know that."

John smiled. "We could pay a surprise visit."

"He wouldn't like that," Bethany warned.

"He wouldn't have to know," John countered.

•••••••••

On the first Saturday of the following month, John, Bethany, and Rodney stood on the dock of the west shore.

"It'll only take about twenty minutes to get across by boat," John assured his friends. "It takes three times that to drive around the lake. By the time Dr. Decker gets to town, buys his supplies, and drives home, we can be to the island and back. Don't you want to see what he's got over there?"

"Yeah," Bethany agreed, jumping down into the boat.

Rodney hesitated, but only for a moment. Then he shrugged and climbed aboard, and the three left the shore.

• • • • • • • • • •

The only way to approach Decker Island was through a boat channel that ran directly into the dense foliage of the east beach. There the kids pulled the boat ashore.

"The house is over there." John pointed toward a two-story brick structure, half hidden by gigantic trees. Rodney tied a line from the boat to the aerial root of a mangrove tree. Only a sliver of sandy beach separated them from the jungle of bizarre green plant life that populated most of the island.

Once at the house, John found an open window on the first floor, and the children slipped inside. The silence pressed in on them like a blanket. The air was heavy and damp.

"I think the lab is downstairs," John whispered. Moving quickly, they found the basement laboratory and began to explore. There seemed to be hundreds of plastic and glass jars filled with samples of plant life gathered from the island and the surrounding lake waters.

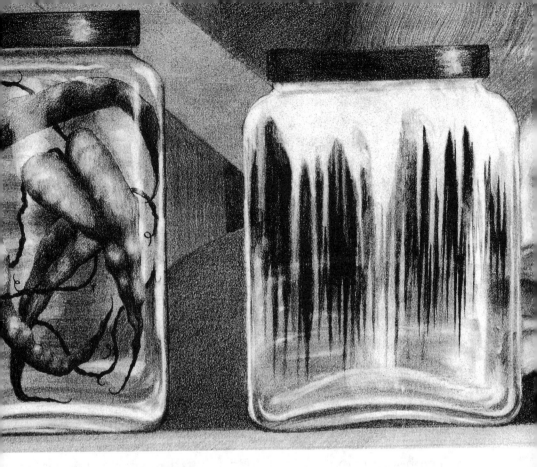

"Yuck!" Rodney held up a vial filled with some disgusting green gook. "What do you think this is?"

"Your lunch," Bethany answered with a devilish grin.

After searching for a while, John gave a deep sigh. "I guess it wasn't really true. I don't see anything here that is all that unusual." He glanced out the window. "It must be getting late. We'd better head back." He walked toward the basement stairs, when Rodney suddenly let out a yelp.

"OWWWW! I stubbed my toe!"

"On what?" John asked. He lifted the wrinkled rug under Rodney's feet. "Look at this!"

A tiny handle stuck up from the floor. It was a part of a

small wooden hatch or door. Tugging on the handle, John gazed down into a dark opening.

"There's another level," he whispered, grabbing a flashlight from a nearby countertop. "Let's see what's down there."

"I get to go first," Rodney demanded. "We wouldn't have found the door if I hadn't stubbed my toe."

John handed over the flashlight, and the trio started down the wooden stairs, the soggy boards creaking under their weight. Once at the bottom, Rodney stepped out onto the concrete floor and shined the flashlight from side to side.

"It's empty," he announced, moving farther into the room. "There isn't a thing here."

John and Bethany stepped down. "The floor feels kind of funny," Bethany observed.

A peculiar slurping sound echoed through the large room. Rodney turned the flashlight toward the ground. "What in the . . . ?" But before he could finish, a thick finger of gooey reddish slime encircled his foot. John watched in stunned silence as the jelly-like ooze slithered up his friend's leg.

Rodney began to beat at the sticky goo with the flashlight. In the rocking beam of light, John could see that the entire floor was covered by a thick layer of the pulsating muck.

"The slime mold!" he screamed. "We've got to get out!" He pushed Bethany back toward the sagging staircase, but when he turned to reach for Rodney, he saw only a quivering mass of crimson slime. From somewhere deep within, his friend uttered a final scream.

John felt a slimy thread grasping at his own ankle. With a cry, he leaped for the stairs and clambered to safety, slamming the trapdoor behind him.

"Let's get out of here!" he shrieked to Bethany. Together they dove through the still-open window and sprinted for the shore. John thought that his heart would burst from the strain. Once on the beach, Bethany fell sobbing to the sand as John worked with shaking hands to free the boat. The tiny craft had drifted farther into the undergrowth and he had to clear away the leaves and vines that clogged their escape. But the harder he worked, the more tangled the boat became.

Suddenly he heard a frantic wail. John lifted his gaze to see Bethany wrapped in a web of vines that hung from a nearby tree. The more she struggled, the more the web tightened.

"Help me, John!" she shrieked.

He jumped up and tried to pull the grasping tendrils away from his friend, but for every vine he grabbed, two more whipped in to take its place. Bethany disappeared before his eyes into a tangle of vegetation. Helplessly, he listened to her last muffled squeals.

With tears flowing down his cheeks, John stared at the boat. It was covered with the deadly vines. Some lay perfectly still. Others twitched slightly as if waiting for him to approach.

John set his face in determination.

"The bridge," he said aloud, remembering how Dr. Decker had once described a low bridge he had built across the bog so that he could drive his four-wheeler to the mainland even during the rainy season.

Setting out for the south side of the island, John didn't take long to reach the escape route . . . or to see that it was impassable. Deadly vines covered every inch of the rough wooden structure. On either side of the bridge stretched several hundred yards of muddy, sopping bog. It was probably filled with snakes and who knows what else, but it was the only way off the island.

Taking a deep breath, John took a step into the muck and sank to his ankles. He tried another step, and another, and even though the water was only about an inch deep, it was almost impossible to move. He was stuck. Pulling up hard on his leg, his foot suddenly wrenched free, but his shoe stayed behind in the dark, stinking mud.

Afraid of what might be waiting unseen in the sludge, John hesitated to take another step.

"This is impossible," he moaned. Then he noticed a pair of huge, oval green leaves that looked as if they were floating just at the surface of the bog. He'd seen leaves like that, but smaller, somewhere before. He couldn't remember where. They looked a little like a gigantic lily pad. He recalled Decker telling him about water lilies in the Amazon jungle that could actually support the weight of a child.

Shading his eyes against the glare of sunlight on the water, he saw that there were several of the lily pad-type plants. They formed an almost continuous, living bridge to the opposite shore.

"It might work," he said to himself with renewed hope. Carefully, he raised his bare foot and stepped onto the plant. It seemed sturdy. John shifted his weight and hoisted himself onto the thick, spongy leaf. It sank a little way into the mud, but it did hold his weight. Slowly and carefully, he worked his way across the bog from leaf to leaf.

I'm going to make it! he thought, allowing a shiver of elation to course through his body. Just a few more yards and he would be on solid ground. He jumped to the next leaf, but his foot slipped out from under him. There was something coating the surface . . . something sticky . . . slimy. Struggling to stand, he slid toward the central vein of the strange double leaf. In a flash, the two halves slammed shut.

"Help!" he cried out to no one. He pushed with all his strength, but the leaves wouldn't budge. Then he tugged at the tough, sword-like spines that were criss-crossed along the edges of his emerald prison. It was no use. With a gurgling sound, a thick, sticky fluid began to bubble up around his ankles. Too late, John remembered where he had seen tiny plants similar to the one that now had him trapped.

"They're not all that special," he had said to Decker. But

now, as the fluid rose higher and higher, he knew that he had been wrong. This Venus's-flytrap was indeed very special . . . and very hungry. He screamed out in terror, but there was no one near to hear.